| B2B | 行銷篇

Speak like a true B2B Marketing Pro

企業英語會話

李純白・著

五南圖書出版公司 印行

Preface 推薦序 1

　　這本書教您用最簡單的英語跟國外客戶談生意，也教您用最文雅的英語跟國外的供應商殺價。

　　用英語跟國外客戶談生意，其實是大部分上班族學英語的終極目標。因為許多上班族努力學英語，目的就是想要找一份薪水比較高的工作，而企業之所以願意花高薪聘請英語比較好的員工，目的就是希望員工能直接用英語跟外國人談生意。

　　然而，許多的上班族雖然對自身的業務十分熟悉，也學過許多年的英語，但是在面對國外客戶或是供應商的時候說不出話來。舉例來說，所有的業務人員都知道報價有多麼的重要，但是卻有許多業務人員不知道「報價」的英語怎麼說？而就算知道了，也往往不知道要怎麼很自然地、主動地向客戶提起報價的事情。

　　再舉個例子來說，所有的採購人員都知道殺價的重要性，但是許多亞洲的採購人員面對國外供應商的時候，卻會吞吞吐吐的說不出話來。因為我們以前在學校學的都是客客氣氣的英語，開口閉口都是「請」、「謝謝」、「對不起」，但是我們在面對國外供應商的時候，總不能這樣溫良恭儉讓吧？

　　目前市面上的商業英語書籍，大多是由英語老師所編寫的，文辭雖然優美，但往往不切實際，一件簡單的事情說的翻來覆去的，卻說不到重點；教材中教了很多複雜的文法句型跟新字彙，但是卻沒有涵蓋國際商務上最常用的一些術語。

李純白老師是我在臺大棒球隊的學長，他從臺大商學系畢業之後，遠赴美國德拉瓦大學取得MBA學位，學有專精，英語非常好，又曾經在跨國公司工作過二十幾年，累積了非常豐富的國際貿易與跨國管理經驗。他寫的這個系列，就是一套專為亞洲人設計的商業英語教材，這套教材避開了艱深難懂的文法句型、不用偏僻冷門的字彙，教您在短時間之內，用最簡單但也最實用英語跟國外的客戶談生意、用最文雅但是強硬的英語跟國外供應商殺價。

　　這個系列原先是以線上教材的形式推出的，結合了我們公司的 MyET 英語學習平臺，讓學生們可以藉由聽跟說的方式，迅速地掌握商業英語的核心能力。而由於這套教材非常的實用，因此在短短的一年之間，已經有十幾家臺灣、中國大陸，以及日本的大學及企業集體採購使用。而這些企業及大學，也一再跟我們反應，希望能有一套相對應的紙本書籍，對教材中的字彙文法做更詳細的解釋、對各種句型的使用時機做更深入的說明。

　　這是一套內行人為專業的商務人士所寫的英語教材，相信您一定會喜歡。

林宣敬

艾爾科技股份有限公司執行長

Preface 推薦序2

　　在世界地球村的今日，跨國的貿易和商業往來也日益頻繁，對商業大學的同學而言，掌握和駕馭商業交易的英語會話實在非常重要。感謝李純白老師能編寫此一本實用的好書，同學們如能好好研讀，當可大幅提升自己的商用英文的程度。

張瑞雄

國立臺北商業大學校長

2014年8月

Preface 推薦序 3

Being successful in building profitable and long term B2B relationships depends on building trust, and this does not happen overnight – it takes a diligent, thorough and professional approach, underpinned by a whole lot of hard work.

想要成功建立長期又能獲利的 B2B 買賣關係，勢必得由建立互信開始。然而 B2B 互信絕非一蹴可幾，得依靠一套結合勤奮不息、周密思考、與高度專業素養為一體的工作方法。

This exact approach was so powerfully demonstrated to me when I first started working with Paul, at a time when he was being challenged with the need to build brand value in the highly competitive Taiwan market. The approach worked, and Paul earned the trust and the respect of the customers and the suppliers.

當我初開始和 Paul 共事時，就強烈感受到這種工作方法的動力。當時，Paul 接下在高度競爭的台灣市場中，建立世界級品牌價值的挑戰。幾年下來，這套方法果真奏效，Paul 贏得客戶與供應廠商共同的尊敬與信任。

Communication between West and East is not as easy as may often be assumed these days – there are many cases where misunderstandings have led to missed opportunities – damaging that trust that is so hard to build. This has not happened in the markets handled by Paul, and again it is fitting that his careful approach is explained in these books for the benefit of others. After all, there is nothing to be gained by re-inventing the wheel, and we can all learn from the experiences of others.

如今東西方之間的溝通並不如我們想像那般容易，一個小小誤解往往就導致喪失大商機。更糟糕的是，還可能危害到辛苦建立起來的互信。然而在Paul所負責的市場裡都未曾發生過這種情況。在這一套書裡，Paul 也詳細說明了上述的工作方法，希望能帶給他人更直接的利益。畢竟很多事情不需非得自行鑽研，我們隨時能夠從別人經驗中吸取到寶貴的現成方法。

In a typically practical manner, this series of books delivers guidance that is based on real life situations and current day conditions. It is entirely logical that students of his work therefore have the opportunity to benefit from his vast array of experience and wisdom, gained at the "coal face"; the "front line"; the "sharp end" through learning and using English.

在這一套書中，Paul 以一種專業又實用的著作方式，依據各種實際的經歷，配合當今的情況，提供專業意見給使用者參考。如此一來，我相信使用這套書的讀者，能從Paul親身在第一線作戰所累積的黑手實務經驗與企業智慧，透過英語的練習，獲得各種企業專業技能。

Andy Royal
Managing Director
Aero Sense Technologies
http://www.aerosensetech.com/index.html

Preface 作者序

　　我自幼就對英文有興趣。最早的記憶是學齡前總愛在空白紙上胡亂塗鴉些誰也看不懂的連體字形，母親因此來問我在寫些甚麼？我回應說：英文字啊！因為當時母親在聽廣播自學英文，家裡總能找到英文教材。耳濡目染之下，喜歡學習英文的興趣不知不覺陪我走過半個世紀。

　　成長於戰後時期，很自然的在上了初中（北市仁愛初中）之後，才開始接觸正規英文教育。初中有幸受教於三位十分出色的英文老師，讓我打下扎實的基礎。高中（北市成功中學）兩位英文老師，更用另類教法延續了我學習英語的熱情。而大一（台灣大學）遇見周樹華老師，則讓我見識到年輕優秀英文老師的實力和魅力。英文之所以能一路陪伴、協助我走過人生最精采的35年，實在要感謝這些良師們的引領及教導。

　　開心順手（口）使用英文是一回事，會想動手寫英語學習的書，又是另一回事，這全是機緣。2012年中偶然在閒聊之間，和學弟林宜敬（艾爾科技創辦人）有了合作開發自學英語數位教材的想法。藉由這機緣，讓我能將35年 B2B 職涯的專業與經驗，結合我的興趣，轉換成一套適合當今企業內部英語訓練使用的教材，短短半年間，完成了 MyET 的 MBA English 教材編寫。在數位教材上市後，進一步增加內容深度與廣度，完成了這套印刷版 B2B 企業英語訓練教材。擴編的

內容讓我能更貼近產業現狀，利用英語對話方式呈現企業內各部門對外溝通的情境，幫助使用者學到更實用的會話與寫作。

本系列書籍內容分成三本，分別是業務（Sales）、行銷（Marketing）、與作業研發（Operations and R&D）。這幾大部門，也是國內製造業裡，最經常使用英文對外聯繫的單位。內容編寫方式，是依據這四大部門對內對外的運作流程（業務），或者針對特定議題及情境（行銷與作業研發），以會話為主軸，輔以字彙、文法、及句型的解釋與示範。希望能利用工作的相似性，引起使用者的共鳴，自然的反覆練習，進而融會貫通並靈活運用在自身的工作上。

學習語言絕無捷徑，選對方法事半功倍。希望藉由貼近產業實務的編寫方式，讓英語學習變得更輕鬆、更自在。

特別感謝雙親，岳父母和家人的支持，尤其是在美國工作的女兒提供許多寶貴建議。感謝遠在英國的好同事 Andy Royal 專業指正，好友陳少君（Paul Chen）、蕭行志、艾爾科技林宜敬、屏東大學施百俊老師以及五南出版編輯團隊的協助。

李純白

Contents 目錄

💬 **推薦序** Preface .... page 001

💬 **作者序** Preface .... page 007

Lesson ① 銷售預算制定 Sales Budgeting *忙碌頭痛時間*

不是湊數字 Mostly guesstimation .... page 001

- 銷售預算：找A咖客戶談 ask for commitment　001
- Marcom預算：廣告參展 ad & trade shows　011

Lesson ② 銷售目標設定 Objective/Target Setting *斤斤計較*

實際期待值 Impossible is nothing .... page 037

- 個別客戶目標：focusing on the 80%　037
- 總公司的期待：tug of war　045

Lesson ③ 市場區隔／標定／定位 Segmentation/Targeting/Positioning

教你如何作戰 What, Where, and How .... page 079

- 市場區隔：segmentation　079
- 標定與定位：targeting & positioning　085

Lesson
④ 產品／技術藍圖 Product/Technology Roadmap
以技術與客戶同步 Design in to grow .... page 115

  • 產品藍圖：roadmap sharing for solid relationship   115
  • 技術藍圖：roadmap for new development   121

Lesson
⑤ 產品組合與開發 Product Mix & Development
整體利益最大化 Maximizing overall benefits .... page 157

  • 產品組合分配：multiple channel management   157
  • 產品開發流程：a systematic way to succeed   165

Lesson
⑥ 定價：競爭與利潤 Competitiveness & Profitability
市佔率與獲利率，孰先？Share or profit? .... page 191

  • 通路定價：pricing for channel   191
  • 全面漲價：General Rate Increase(GRI)   198

Lesson
⑦ 通路建立與夥伴關係 Channel Building & Relationships
互信互利減少衝突 Mutual trust and benefits .... page 221

  • 通路管理：channel management   221
  • 通路與直接客戶：channel & direct accounts   229

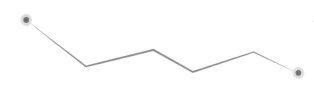

Lesson ⑧ 廣告與參展 Advertising & Exhibition *數位或傳統*

線上離線一起來 Online ad and offline exhibitions .... page 257

● 合作廣告與參展：co-op ad & trade shows   **257**

● 展會現場：at the show   **265**

 **Summary 1**

Annual sales budgeting is one of the most important, yet tedious, jobs for marketing and sales people, particularly in B2B mode. A complete sales budget serves multiple purposes. It defines the sales objectives that the salespeople are to achieve in the coming fiscal year. Accordingly, sales managers assign individual sales targets to each and every salesperson. Then, each salesperson will hold discussions with his or her major accounts (mostly tier 1 and tier 2) to determine the business prospects for the coming year. The sales budget will also become the base on which many business decisions such as capacity planning and capital expenditures are made. Therefore, the sales budget is just too important to ignore. Most businesses start the budgeting process as early as September and complete it by December of each year.

年度銷售預算編列，尤其是在 B2B 模式裡，一直是行銷或業務人員每年最重要的工作之一。編制銷售預

算有多重目的，首要在於確定公司來年的各項銷售目標。業務經理根據這份公司整體銷售目標，分派個人年度銷售目標給每位負責的業務人員身上。接下來，每位業務人員根據自己的銷售目標，回頭和手中各主要客戶（80/20 原理的 20% 客戶群）商討如何達成個別的銷售目標。另外，許多公司的重大決策與規劃，例如產能規劃與資本投資計劃，主要也是依據這份總銷售目標來制定。可見銷售預算的重要性。也因此，多數大型企業的預算制定，從每年九月就開始，一直到十二月才能定案（假設會計年度為 1 至 12 月）。

銷售預算：找 A 咖客戶談 ask for commitment 1-1

Jenny：**Senior M&S Manager, Lyndon Sensing (U.S.A)**：
資深行銷業務經理，美國

Steve：**Sales Manager, Willie Co., Ltd. (Taiwan)**：業務經
理，臺灣

Jenny：Hi Steve, how have you been doing? It's our budget time now, so I need to discuss with you about our business next year.

嗨 Steve，最近好嗎？現在我們要開始製作預算，我得和你討論明年的業務。

Steve：Yes, it's about time to do it. We are also working on our own budgets for the next year. It's really kind of tedious.

是啊，差不多是時候了，我們也在做明年的預算。真的挺麻煩的。

Jenny：I agree. However, it is very important for both of us to have a clear business picture of the coming year. Not only can we get a better understanding of the market prospect in the coming year, but we can also have a clearer indicator for our operations, such as capacity planning.

同意。不過，若能更清楚未來一年的業務狀況，對我們都很重要，不但更能了解市場前景，同時也可以做為公司的重要規劃指標，比方說產能規劃。

Steve：I understand. We also do the same with our end customers. The problem is the numbers they gave to us were never accurate.

And in return, the numbers we give to you could be inaccurate too. It seems there's little we can do about that.

這我了解，我們也得和終端客戶一起做預算。問題是，這些客戶提供的數據從來沒準過。反過頭來，我們給你們的數據也有可能不準確。對於這種現象，我們似乎也束手無策。

Jenny: I share the same concerns with you. But a business partner like your company is just too important to not serve well. You're among our top five customers worldwide, just for your information.

我和你同樣煩惱。不過像你們這樣重要的生意夥伴，我們一定得做好這件事才行。說給你做參考，貴公司是我們全球排名前五大的客戶之一。

Steve: Oh really? That's nice. OK, we'll work closely with you regarding this.

真的嗎？太讚了！好的，我們會密切配合，做好年度銷售預算。

Jenny: Thanks so much. I'll send you some forms to make it easier for you. Call me if you have any questions.

多謝。我會傳一些表格給你，方便你們做事。有問題的話，儘管打電話給我。

1 yet：但是、然而

The Chinese New Year holiday should be fun to most people, yet we were busier than ever.

對多數人來說，春節年假應該最開心的；然而我們卻是忙到不行。

2 tedious：沉悶累人的、冗長乏味的

Julie, a customer review meeting can be tedious, yet I'm sure you'll benefit from it.

客戶檢討會很累人，不過那一定對妳有益處

3 B2B mode：B2B 模式

B2B 爲 Business-to-Business 縮寫。

4 serves multiple purposes：有多重目的

片語 serve a purpose 指「用來達成一個目的」。multiple 多重的。

5 define：定義

The way we support each other cannot be defined by HR's job description of each team member.

人資的工作說明是無法解釋我們團隊成員相互支援的工作方式。

6 sales objective：銷售目標、業務目標

7 achieve：達到、達成

We have a set of tough sales objectives to achieve next year.

明年我們得達成一些很困難的業務目標。

NOTE

⑧ **fiscal year**：會計年度、財政年度

⑨ **accordingly**：因此

We just had a power outage. The production lines stopped accordingly.

剛才停電，因此我們產線停機。

⑩ **assign**：指派、指定、分派

Sandy, no worries. We've assigned William to fix your problem.

別擔心，我們已指派 William 去解決你們的問題了。

no worries 同 don't worry，用於口語。

⑪ **tier 1、tier 2 (accounts)**：第一階、第二階（客戶）

⑫ **prospect for**：對…的展望、前景

Mark, the prospect for Q3 isn't looking good.

Mark，Q3 展望看起來很不妙。

⑬ **capacity planning**：產能規劃

From a long-term point of view, capacity planning is so critical to our competitive position in the industry.

從長期觀點來看，產能規劃對我們的產業競爭地位極為重要。

⑭ **capital expenditure**：資本支出

We will have a tremendous amount of capital expenditure in the new production process next year.

我們明年在新製程上將有巨額的資本支出。

⑮ ignore：忽視、忽略、不顧

Emily, you'd better not ignore the importance of our regular forecast.

Emily，妳最好不要忽視定期預估的重要性。

⑯ as early as：早在

Ethan joined the company as early as 1980.

Ethan 早在 1980 年時就進公司了。

⑰ budget time：（編製）預算時間

西方歐美國家，大多在第三季末，就開始製作來年預算。

⑱ it's about time：該是時候了

也可直接用 it's time。記得 that 後面動詞用過去式，代表早該行動了。

It's about time that we discussed your trip plan.

該來討論你的出差計畫了。

⑲ work on：做某件事情

Ryan, I'll help you work on your presentation soon.

Ryan，我很快會來協助你做簡報資料。

⑳ kind of tedious：有點繁瑣

"kind of" 有些、有點。常在口語會話中使用。

NOTE

㉑ **not only …but (also)**：不但……而且

Not only will Jacob visit the show but he will also attend the symposium.

Jacob 不但會去參觀展覽，他也會參加研討會。

Not only Kenneth but also Margaret will attend the seminar.

不單單 Kenneth 會去，連 Margaret 也會去參加研討會。

Joseph will not only attend the symposium but he will also visit our channel partners.

Joseph 不但會參加研討會，也會去拜訪我們的通路夥伴。

㉒ **indicator**：指標、指示

在這裡也可說是信號 signal。

The decreasing ASP is actually an indicator of the intensifying competition.

一路下滑的平均售價實際上代表競爭正持續加劇當中。

ASP 為 Average Selling Price 的縮寫。

㉓ **do the same**：做同一件事，指編預算

㉔ **accurate**：精確的、準確的

也可說 precise。

㉕ **in return**：回報、回頭來

I taught Steve Office PowerPoint this morning. In return, he helped me with Office Excel in the afternoon.

今天早上我教 Steve 用 Office PowerPoint，他下午教我用 Excel 作為回報。

㉖ **inaccurate**：不精確的、不準確的

也可說 imprecise。

㉗ **it seems**⋯：似乎、看起來

也可說 it appears⋯。

Ella, it seems to me that you offered too many MSPs to your customers.

Ella，看來妳報了太多最低售價給妳的客戶了。

MSP 是 Minimum Selling Price 的縮寫。

㉘ **I share the same concerns with you**：我和你一樣煩惱

㉙ **worldwide**：全世界的、全球的

也可說 throughout the world。

Lucas, currently we have 48 channel partners worldwide.

Lucas，目前我們全球共有 48 家通路夥伴。

NOTE

30 for your information：提供資訊讓你參考

也可說 for your reference。

For your information Hannah, we're developing a new OCXO for radar applications.

Hannah，提供妳參考，我們正在開發一顆雷達用的 OCXO。

31 Oh really?：啊，是這樣子嗎？

日常口語會話的常用語。

課文重點② Summary 2

Recently we've seen and heard "Marcom" a lot more than in the past. Particularly for most industrial firms, Marcom focuses mainly on marketing communications such as PR, advertising, exhibition, and web marketing.

The other three Ps of the marketing mix, namely, "Product", "Price", and "Place" fall into product marketing or even the sales function instead. Product marketing focuses mainly on new product planning and development roadmap, product pricing, as well as channel building and management. As web marketing has been gaining much more weight from the traditional offline marketing, many companies began to adopt different web-based marketing software such as lead management and marketing automation to help create more business opportunities. Inbound marketing has quickly become an important marketing strategy to many companies and has been allocated more company resources than ever before.

近期以來，愈來愈多企業，尤其是大型上市櫃公司，開始採用行銷溝通（Marcom）的企業功能，取代以往的行銷（marketing）部門，以便更精確界定行銷在產業中所扮演的角色。特別對許多科技和工業產品來說，最重要的行銷功能，是新產品開發藍圖（road-map）。而與產品開發息息相關的產品定價，也因此一併納入產品行銷（product marketing）範圍。許多公司甚至將產品行銷功能直接併入業務部門，確保執行效果。另外，科技與工業產品的行銷通路功能，也經常被併入業務部門，統籌運作管理。相較之下，傳統消費產品的行銷重點，如廣告、促銷、包裝、與公關等工作，對於科技與工業產品來說，較難產生直接效果。也因此，這些行銷功能的重要性，就遠不及產品行銷、通路、與客戶關係管理。儘管如此，還是得有專人負責行銷溝通的規劃、執行、考核、與控管，行銷溝通（Marcom）部門也就應運而生。而近年來快速走紅的網路行銷，工作性質以內容為核心，配合CRM 與行銷自動化軟體，形成內向式行銷系統，有別於傳統行銷單位而獨立作業。不過，在多數中小型企業裡，網路行銷工作還是交由 Marcom 負責。

Marcom 預算：廣告參展 ad & trade shows 1-2

Anita : **Marcom Manager, Wilcox Tech (Singapore)**；
Marcom 經理，新加坡

George : **Sales Manager, Wilcox Tech (Singapore)**：業務經
理，新加坡

Anita : Hi George, <u>you got a minute</u>? I think <u>we'd better</u> sit down and start reviewing the Marcom budget of the coming year.

嗨 George，可以打擾一下嗎？我們最好坐下來開始看看明年行 Marcom 的預算。

 Dr. Lee 解析

這裡，You got a minute？並不是問有沒有一分鐘，而是「可以打擾你一下下嗎？」的意思。

George : Oh yes, Anita, we need to do it ASAP. We will be <u>playing a whole new ball game</u> next year. We need <u>a lot more</u> support from you.

是啊 Anita，我們得儘早做。明年我們業務會面臨很不一樣的局面，需要靠妳們多幫忙。

Dr. Lee 解析

> George 的業務部門明年將面臨極大的壓力，希望 Marcom 能多編些預算提供協助。

Anita：Great, how about we <u>meet up</u> in your office at two o'clock this afternoon?

很好啊。那今天下午兩點鐘，我來你辦公室談如何？

Dr. Lee 解析

> 編預算是大事，這二位主管隨即敲定碰面時間。

George：OK, I'll be waiting for you. Kim, my senior sales manager, will also attend.

OK，我等你。我們的資深業務經理 Kim 也會參加。

Dr. Lee 解析

> 實際負責編預算的是業務經理 Kim，所以 George 也一併請 Kim 參加。

Anita：Hi George, hi Kim, good afternoon. We'd better start now.

嗨 George，嗨 Kim，午安。我們現在就開始吧。

Dr. Lee 解析

預算協商會議多是開門見山，直來直往。

George : Right, what Marcom resource will we get from you next year? <u>Same as</u> this year?

好。那明年 Marcom 能給我們什麼資源？和今年一樣嗎？

Dr. Lee 解析

業務部門劈頭就問 Marcom，來年能夠支援什麼。

Anita : Well, we'll have a new <u>focus</u> next year. We'll put a lot more efforts on web marketing projects than on <u>conventional marketing</u> activities such as <u>trade shows</u> and <u>printed literatures</u>.

明年我們會有不同的重點，相較於傳統的行銷活動，如參展和平面文宣，我們明年將會投注更多心力在網路行銷上面。

Dr. Lee 解析

Marcom 來年的重點，將由傳統離線式行銷，轉移到網路行銷上。

George : Web marketing? You mean internet marketing? It sounds interesting, but I <u>have no idea</u> how it will help us get more business.

網路行銷？你是指網際網路行銷？聽起來很有趣，不過我不了解網路行銷如何能幫我們多拿一些生意。

Dr. Lee 解析

業務部門對網路行銷雖不陌生，卻高度懷疑網路行銷能幫業務多做多少生意。

Anita: Yeah, I guess we sales and marketing need to discuss it in detail. After all, web marketing is so new to us.

對，我認為業務和行銷得好好討論才行。畢竟我們對網路行銷還很陌生。

Dr. Lee 解析

就如同許多行銷部門那樣，Marcom 往往搞不清楚第一線業務需要什麼。雙方面對面舌戰一番，似乎無法避免。

George: Anita, you have to understand that we were assigned with a set of sales objectives next year that are too tough, if not impossible, to achieve. We do need sufficient and effective marketing support from Marcom.

Anita，你得了解，我們明年背負著幾項幾乎不可能達成的業務目標。需要你們提供充足而且有效的支援。

Dr. Lee 解析

> 業務永遠有個好理由要求外部支援，那就是來年的超高業務目標。

Anita : I know clearly what your objectives are and I fully under-stand your position. That's the reason why management has been asking us to fully support you. <u>Nevertheless</u>, we only have limited budget.

我很清楚你們明年的業務目標，也很了解業務的立場。這也正是上面一直要求我們要全力支援業務部門的原因。不過，我們的預算很有限。

Dr. Lee 解析

> Marcom 似乎只有說場面話的份，然後以預算有限做回應。

George : I guess unless you're <u>in my position</u>, you won't be able to know <u>exactly</u> how tough it is to <u>achieve</u> our goals. We're talking about 50%, even 60% sales growth for next year. We never had such a tough <u>task</u> to <u>accomplish</u> before.

我想，除非妳親身體驗，不然很難了解那是多棘手的業務目標。明年我們營收得成長 50%，甚至 60% 啊！那是一項空前困難的任務。

Dr. Lee 解析

業務還是不認為 Marcom 真正了解他們所承受的壓力，還是一再訴苦。

Anita：Believe me, George. I do understand the <u>tremendous</u> pressure your team is going to <u>endure</u>. We'll work closely with you to <u>maximize the ROI</u> of our marketing efforts.

請相信我，George。我絕對理解你們團隊所承受的沉重壓力。Marcom 會和各位一起努力，以便獲取最佳的投資報酬。

Dr. Lee 解析

Marcom 不斷釋出善意，卻也不忘透露投資報酬率 ROI 的重要性。

George：OK, I'm glad to hear that, but please show us what we're going to get from Marcom <u>in terms of</u> trade shows, advertising, literatures, and what you have just said, the web marketing programs.

那很好，不過請告訴我，我們明年在參展、廣告、文宣，還有妳剛才講的網路行銷等方面，Marcom 如何能協助我們？

Dr. Lee 解析

> 業務要求 Marcom 具體說明，來年在參展、廣告、與網路行銷等活動細節。

Anita : I'll start with the web marketing. First, we will have a new website by the end of Q2 next year. It will be <u>a lot easier</u> for visitors to <u>get access to</u> the information they want. More importantly, we will be able to <u>convert</u> the visits into viable <u>sales leads</u> more effectively.

我先說網路行銷好了，首先我們在明年 Q2 末期就會有個新網站，使用者很容易就能找到所需要的資訊。更重要的是，瀏覽轉換率將大大提升。

Dr. Lee 解析

> Marcom 當然先說來年的重點任務。重點放在轉換率（conversion），從造訪瀏覽數（visits）轉化成銷售線索（qualified sales leads）。試圖以改善轉換率，解開長久以來導致雙方對立的最大心結。

George : Recently, I've heard of some marketing automation software with <u>so-called</u> <u>sales funnel</u> design, which is capable of generating useful sales leads effectively. Is that what you're talking about?

最近我有聽過一些行銷自動化軟體，內建所謂銷售漏斗的設計，妳說的是這個嗎？

Dr. Lee 解析

一般來說，行銷自動化軟體多以銷售線索 sales leads 管理為核心。使用起來效果如何，業務還是沒太大信心。

Anita : Yes, sales lead management is the core of marketing automation and it will be an important part of our phase 2 project. But first things first, a new and much more inbound oriented website will be installed by the end of Q2 next year.

沒錯，銷售線索管理是行銷自動化的核心，也是我們第二階段最重要的工作。不過更重要的，是明年 Q2 底架設完成的全新內向式網站。

Dr. Lee 解析

這點 Marcom 想法是循序漸進的，在引進行銷自動化之前，公司得先砍掉現有網站，重新設計內向（inbound）導向的網站。

George : I'm not sure how it will help us get more business. I have the same doubts with the CRM that we use every day.

我不清楚新網站能如何幫助我們擴增業務，我也懷疑我們天天在用的 CRM 軟體到底有什麼用處。

Dr. Lee 解析

> 業務之所以對於行銷自動化的功效打問號，主要是對於一些行銷軟體，如 CRM 功能的懷疑。

Anita: Don't worry, George. We realize how you salespeople think about web marketing. There will be sufficient training for sales before implementing. Meanwhile, we will <u>implement</u> it in <u>three phases</u>. You'll have sufficient time to <u>become more familiarized</u> before advancing to the next phase. Anyway, we will make sure you guys <u>feel comfortable</u> with it from beginning to the end.

George，別擔心。我們了解業務人員對網路行銷的看法。在正式上線之前，一定會有足夠的教育訓練。同時我們會分三階段上系統，讓業務人員有足夠時間來熟悉系統循序漸進。無論如何，我們會確保各位從頭到尾都能輕鬆應對。

Dr. Lee 解析

> Marcom 要導入並推動網路行銷，既要有策略，也要有手段。否則不但事倍功半，還會引發內部衝突及投資失敗。

George: I really hope so. <u>We'll see.</u> Now we should start discussing the <u>conventional</u> Marcom programs that we need for the next year. The most important events are the two trade shows, one in Las Vegas and the other in Tokyo. Are they in your budget?

真希望如此，到時就知道。現在我們應該開始討論明年我們需要的傳統行銷方案了吧？最重要的是拉斯維加斯和東京的兩個展覽，你們有編進預算裡嗎？

Dr. Lee 解析

業務所關心的，往往是比較短期的績效。因此對於 Marcom 的要求，還是聚焦在來年的參展，希望 Marcom 能全力支援。

Anita : George, I'm afraid that only one will be <u>approved</u> as a result of the tight budget. Moreover, we found neither shows <u>justifiable</u> while calculating the ROI. I <u>suggest</u> that you carefully review the necessity of the shows and adjust accordingly.

George，由於預算卡得緊，恐怕你們只能參加一個展。而且 ROI 算下來，這二個展都划不來。我建議你們再仔細研究參展的必要性，並做出調整。

Dr. Lee 解析

由於立場並不一致，Marcom 往往只能滿足部份業務的需求。也大都以投資報酬率（ROI）不佳為理由砍預算。

George : Look Anita, I <u>disagree with</u> you on this. These two shows are much bigger than the two we attended this year. And more importantly, both are <u>dedicated trade shows</u> for our products. We <u>rely on</u> them to promote our new systems. I would <u>insist</u> Marcom <u>allocate</u> sufficient budget to these two shows.

Anita，我不同意你這個說法。這兩個展的規模，要比今年我們參加的那兩個展大得多。更重要的是，這些都是最適合的專業展，我們得靠這兩個展推廣我們的新系統。我得堅持你們Marcom 替這二個展準備足夠的預算。

Dr. Lee 解析

業務當然不會輕易妥協，再次強調所提需求的絕對必要性，並強硬表態。

Anita：All right, George, I got your point. I'll further investigate your request quickly and come back to you tomorrow. However, I might need some more inputs from you guys for evaluation.

好吧，George，我了解你的意思，我會立刻再研究看看，明天回覆你。不過可能還得請你們提供更多資訊，以便評估。

Dr. Lee 解析

一旦陷入討論僵局，雙方大多會採取協商方式，各自重新檢討，決定取捨。

George：No problem with that. Just let us know what you want and we'll send it to you ASAP.

沒問題，你需要什麼資料儘管說，我們一定儘快提供。

Dr. Lee 解析

業務立場很清楚，也保持修正彈性。

Anita：Since our budget is <u>tight and limited</u>, very likely we'll have no more money for advertising or other promotional stuff.

受限於我們緊縮的預算，我們很可能就沒有多餘的錢來做廣告和其它促銷活動。

Dr. Lee 解析

同樣，Marcom 也會做出必要調整。

George：I got it. We don't worry too much about them. We only need money for these two trade shows.

了解。我們不擔心那些，只需要這兩個展的預算就夠了。

Dr. Lee 解析

結束前，業務再次強調自己的底線。

NOTE

❶ Marcom：行銷溝通

marketing communications 的縮寫。

❷ a lot more：更多

也可說 much more。

❸ PR：公關

❹ advertising：廣告

❺ exhibition：展覽、展會

❻ web marketing：網路行銷

❼ promotion：促銷、推廣

❽ fall into：屬於、落入

Based on what you just described, I believe the problem falls into mechanical design instead of sensor selection.

根據你所描述，我認為問題出在機械設計而不是選錯感應器。

❾ roadmap：藍圖、路徑圖

Product roadmap planning is one of the major tasks for an industrial marketer.

產品藍圖規劃是工業行銷人員主要工作之一。

NOTE

⑩channel：通路

Channel sales account for approximately 30% of our total revenue.

通路生意大約占了我們總營收的三成。

⑪offline marketing：離線行銷

指傳統行銷，相對於線上行銷（online marketing）或網路行銷（web marketing）。

⑫adopt：採用、採行

Michael's suggestion to adopt inbound marketing strategy was refused by the board.

Michael 建議採行內向式行銷策略被董事會拒絕了。

⑬web-based：網路上運作的

Our web-based CRM system helps to improve the productivity of most salespeople.

我們以網路運作的 CRM 系統，協助改善了多數銷售人員的生產力。

⑭lead management：銷售線索管理

Lead management function is the core of marketing automation system.

銷售線索管理功能是行銷自動化系統的核心。

⑮marketing automation：行銷自動化

NOTE

⑯ **inbound marketing**：內向式行銷

The core concept of inbound marketing is to help potential customers find you more effectively through the internet.

內向式行銷的核心概念：運用網路協助潛在客戶更有效找到供應廠商。

⑰ **ever before**：以往任何時候、以往

Sonia, nowadays customers are a lot more demanding than ever before.

Sonia，現今的客戶比以往任何時候更挑剔、更苛求。

⑱ **you got a minute?**：你有一點時間嗎？

多指很短時間。

⑲ **we'd better**：我們最好

是 we had better 的縮寫。

Laura, we'd better call the courier to see where the shipment is now.

Laura，我們最好打電話問快遞，看看那批貨現在是在哪裡。

⑳ **play a whole new ball game**：一個完全不同的情況

意指不同的競爭局面。

Once we launch the G4 instruments, we'll be playing a different ball game.

一旦 G4 儀器上市，競爭態勢就會完全不同了。

NOTE

㉑**a lot more**：更多的

同 *much more*。

Luke, considering the individual contribution to our company, Baxton is a lot more important than Dell.

Luke，若考慮對公司的個別貢獻度，Baxton 比 Dell 還重要得多。

㉒**meet up**：碰面、碰頭

Amelia, why don't we meet up later around noon at Corner Coffee?

Amelia，我們何不在今天中午到 Corner Coffee 見面呢？

㉓**(the) same as**：與…相同

口語中 *the* 省略了。

Nathan, what was the transducer that WTE used for its agitator system? Same as our KIS beams?

Nathan，WTE 的攪拌系統是用哪種傳感器？和我們 KIS 樑式相同嗎？

㉔**focus (名)**：聚焦、焦點

㉕**conventional marketing**：傳統式行銷，又稱離線式行銷 **offline marketing**。

㉖**trade shows**：展覽會

㉗**printed literature**：印刷文宣

指產品型錄，或公司介紹等相關印刷品。

NOTE

㉘ **have no idea**：不知道、不明白、不清楚

Samantha, I don't have any idea of when the next roadmap meeting is.

Samantha，我不知道下次藍圖會議何時開。

㉙ **I guess**：我認為、我想

㉚ **in detail**：詳細、仔細

Felix, we have to review the issue in detail.

Felix，我們得仔細檢討這件事。

㉛ **after all**：畢竟

Let's move on to the next topic. After all, this one is too minor to waste everybody's time.

我們繼續下面的議題吧！畢竟這議題不那麼重要，沒必要浪費各位寶貴時間。

㉜ **if not impossible**：如果不是不可能

換言之，「即便是可能，也是…」。

Richard, it's too difficult, if not impossible, to dismantle the testers now.

Richard，現在要拆掉測試機，就算是可能，也會非常困難。

㉝ **sufficient and effective**：充足且有效的

NOTE

㉞nevertheless：不過、然而

Hey, I know you guys are not happy with the recent workload. Nevertheless, we still have to finish all these before we can call it a day.

各位，我了解大家對最近工作繁重不太開心，然而我們還是得做完這些才能收工。

call it a day 收工、到此為止、不再做下去。

㉟in my position：我的立場

David, I believe you would do the same if you were in my position.

David，換做是你，我相信你也會這麼做。

㊱exactly：全然的、完全的、確切的

Patrick, about the incident, it seems to me things are not exactly as you said.

Patrick，關於那事件，好像不完全像你說的那樣。

㊲achieve：達成、實現

Jason, very good Q1 performance. Yet you still have a tougher goal to achieve.

Jason，Q1 你表現真好。不過你還得達成一個更困難的目標。

㊳task：任務、使命、工作

NOTE

㊴ accomplish：完成、實現

Lillian, it's impossible to accomplish the mission assigned to us without a miracle.

Lillian 若沒奇蹟出現，我們不可能完成使命。

㊵ tremendous：很大的、巨大的

Because of the recent slump, Simon has been under tremendous pressure from the headquarters.

由於最近業績大幅下滑，Simon 承受來自總公司極大的壓力。

㊶ endure：忍受、忍耐

I'm worrying how much longer Olivia's going to endure this pressure.

我擔心 Olivia 還會忍受多久這壓力。

㊷ ensure：確保

㊸ maximize the ROI：獲取最高投資報酬率

ROI 是 Return On Investment 的縮寫。

㊹ in terms of：以…來說、在…方面

Stainless steel 17-4 PH is superior to stainless 316 in terms of strength.

在強度上，17-4 PH 不鏽鋼要優於 316 不鏽鋼。

㊺ a lot easier：容易的多

The expense budget is a lot easier to make than the sales budget.

編制費用預算要比編制銷售預算容易多了。

NOTE

46 get access to：獲得、獲取

With this new approved model, we'll be able to get access to a more profitable market segment.

有了這認證新機種，我們就有機會打入一塊高利潤市場了。

47 convert：轉換、轉化

convert A into B：將 A 轉化成 B。

In order to get results, marketing people first have to convert leads into prospects.

行銷人員必須先將線索轉換成潛在客戶，才能得到結果。

48 sales leads：銷售線索

Qualified sales leads are always what salespeople prefer to receive the most.

篩選過的優質線索永遠是業務人員的最愛。

49 so-called：所謂的

50 sales funnel：銷售漏斗

Attract visits, qualify and nurture them into leads, develop leads into prospects, and convert prospects into customers; these are the most important actions along the sales funnel.

銷售漏斗裡最重要的行動依序為：吸引瀏覽客，篩選並培養成為線索，再進一步開發線索為潛在客戶，最後轉換成客戶。

NOTE

51 first things first：先解決（討論、談）最重要的事

OK, first things first, check your e-mails to see if there's any new booking.

好，重要事先來：各位查一下 e-mail 看看有沒有新訂單。

52 inbound oriented：內向式（行銷）導向的

In the era of internet, inbound oriented design concept is definitely essential.

在網路年代，內向式導向的設計概念是絕對必要的。

53 install：安裝

Matthew is going to install a new temperature test machine in our lab later today.

今天稍晚，Matthew 將在我們實驗室裡安裝溫度測試機臺。

54 CRM：**Customer Relationship Management**（客戶關係管理）的縮寫

55 implement：實施、執行

Hannah, you'd better get ready for the upcoming GRI to be implemented next Monday.

Hannah，你最好準備應付下星期一開始實施的漲價。

GRI 為 General Rate Increase 的縮寫。

56 three phases：三階段

NOTE

57 become more familiarized：變得更熟悉、更熟識、更了解

Jim, I need at least two days to become more familiarized with the new ERP system.

Jim，我至少需要兩天弄熟這套新 ERP 系統。

ERP 為 Enterprise Resource Planning 的縮寫，即企業資源規劃系統。

58 feel comfortable：感到自在、舒服

Linda, let me know if you don't feel comfortable with the design.

Linda，如果妳覺得設計有任何不對勁，儘管告訴我。

59 we'll see：再看吧、到時便知的意思

So Owen, this is the best you can get from TAB? OK, we'll see.

Owen，這就是 TAB 能給我們最大的訂單配額？好，再看吧！

60 conventional：傳統的

也可說 traditional。

61 approved：經承認過的、經准許過的

Daniel told me all our samples had been approved by their R&D engineers.

Daniel 告訴我，所有樣品都通過他們研發工程師認證了。

62 as a result of：因為、由於

As a result of the raw material shortage, we were forced to pay a premium price to get enough of them for production.

由於原料短缺，我們被迫付高價買到足夠的量，以應付生產所需。

NOTE

63 justifiable：有充分、正當理由的

Grace, your request for output matching is not justifiable.

Grace，妳要求輸出匹配的理由並不充分。

64 suggest：建議

注意：後面子句裡動詞必須用原形動詞。

Anita, I suggest that you offer a price that is higher than ASP.

Anita，我建議妳報一個比 ASP 稍高的價錢。

65 disagree with：不同意、持不同意見

Sorry Larry, I disagree with you on the issue of system accuracy.

抱歉 Larry，我不同意你對系統精度的說法。

66 dedicated trade shows：專業展覽

67 rely on：依賴、依靠

The OEM orders didn't look good. We'll have to rely on channel business in Q2 and Q3.

OEM 訂單看起來不妙，我們 Q2 和 Q3 得依賴通路生意了。

68 insist：堅持

不同句型練習，

片語 insist on：

Joan insists on working on the night shift.

Joan 堅持要上夜班。

insist 接子句用原形動詞：

Andrew insists that FAE go with him. (should省略)

Andrew 堅持 FAE 和他一同前去。

NOTE

⑥⑨**allocate**：分配、配給

Since we only have limited capacity in September and October, we'll have to allocate among those AAA customers.

由於九、十兩個月產能有限,我們得分配給幾家 AAA 大咖客戶。

⑦⓪**investigate**：調查、研究

Dennis, we're sorry for the shipping mistake. We'll investigate right away and make sure it won't happen again.

Dennis,出貨失誤真是很抱歉,我們會立刻調查原因並且保證絕不再犯。

⑦①**evaluation**：評估、審核

Emma, don't forget we'll meet tomorrow morning for your mid-year performance evaluation.

Emma,別忘了明天上午我們得進行上半年的績效評核。

⑦②**tight and limited**：緊縮又受限

銷售目標設定
Objective/Target Setting

 **Summary 1**

Setting up sales goals or sales objectives is crucial to the annual sales budget. The objectives show how the company expects the sales team to perform for the coming year. It is a rather time-consuming process, especially in a large global company with operations in different regions or countries. Regardless of the method, top-down or bottom-up, setting up sales goals takes lots of discussions and negotiations among parties in headquarters, branches, sales teams, and all team members. In the real business world, annual sales objectives are always unrealistically tough, if not totally impossible, to achieve. Basically, sales objectives include sales income, sales volume, profit margin, new business income, the number of new customers, and many others such as Average Selling Price (ASP) and contribution of tier 1 customers.

年度銷售目標制訂，是年度銷售預算的重頭戲之一。銷售目標代表了公司最高經營者的企圖心，以及對整個業務團隊的期望與要求。編製銷售預算之所以費時

費力，主要就是卡在目標設定上。無論是自上而下，或由下而上的方式，尤其在跨國性大型企業裡，各階層業務單位的垂直討論與溝通協調，往往曠日廢時。對業務人員來說，年度銷售目標永遠都屬極高難度，甚至是不可能的任務。幾項常見的銷售目標，包括銷售金額、銷售數量、利潤率、新增客戶營收、新增客戶數目、以及其他目標，如平均銷售價格、以及第一階客戶貢獻度等等。

個別客戶目標：focusing on the 80%   2-1

Jenny ： **Senior M&S Manager, Lyndon Sensing (U.S.A)**：
資深行銷業務經理，美國

Steve ： **Sales Manager, Willie Co., Ltd. (Taiwan)**：業務經
理，臺灣

Video conference 視訊會議

Jenny ： Hi Steve, are you ready to discuss the budget now?

嗨 Steve，準備好來討論預算了嗎？

Steve ： Hi Jenny, I guess so as I just finished "guesstimation", I mean
half by guessing and half by estimating.

嗨 Jenny，大概可以了，我剛剛才湊出數字來。我的意思是半
猜測半估算啦！

Jenny ： I see. We'll see what we can do for a mutual understanding.
Let's begin with form A, budget by product category and
model.

這樣啊，我們來看看能不能達成共識。先從 A 表格開始，依照
產品類別及型號來做。

Steve ： OK, the numbers you see are what we'll be able to achieve
with full effort. What do you think?

好，你所看到的數字，是我們盡全力才能做到的狀況。你覺得
如何？

Jenny : In general, they look quite good except for Display model SHS 1104, SHM 3381, and THS 2337. We are expecting much higher volume.

大體來說，除了顯示器型號 SHS1104、SHM3381、和 THS2337 外，其他看起來都很好。我們期望能有更高的數量。

Steve : You're scaring me, how much higher?

別嚇我，你們期望是有多高？

Jenny : Up by 25%. We need that number to maximize our capacity utilization.

要高出 25%，我們需要這個量來拉高產能利用率。

Steve : OK, I got your point. But then we will have to adjust the selling prices.

好，我了解你的意思。不過如果是那樣，我們就得調整售價了。

Jenny : That is workable. We'll further talk about it. Regarding form B, the Monthly Budget, you'll be OK if those three figures are revised to our expectation.

可行，我們再來談。關於 B 表格月預算，如果那三個數字能修正到我們預期的量，就沒問題了。

NOTE

① set up：設定、設立、建立

Setting up annual sales objectives is a tough job for all marketing and sales people.

設定年度銷售目標對每一位行銷及業務人員來說，都是一件很困難的事。

② goal：目標

多指較長程的目標。

③ objective：目標、目的

多指較短程的目標。

④ crucial：重要的、有決定性的

Nicholas, the OCXO under development for Femtocell is crucial to us, particularly to tier 2 sales.

Nicholas，那顆還在研發，要用在 Femtocell 的 OCXO 對我們很重要，尤其是對第二階市場的營收。

⑤ time-consuming：耗時的、費時的

To obtain a design-in from customers like Arrow or Dexton is always time-consuming.

要從 Arrow 或 Dexton 這種公司拿到設計承認都是很費時的。

⑥ especially：特別地

也可說 particularly。

Mia, be especially cautious with that instrument.

Mia，使用那臺儀器時請特別小心。

NOTE

❼regardless：無論、不管

We'll achieve our sales objectives regardless of a few setbacks in bidding.

儘管幾次標案砸鍋，我們還是會達成銷售目標。

❽top-down：由上至下

由高層經理決定目標後向下頒布要求執行。

❾bottom-up：由下至上

由部門基層討論形成目標後向上呈報。

Either top-down or bottom-up, it's all about negotiations.

無論是從上到下或由下至上，重點都是來回不斷協商。

❿headquarters：總部、總公司

多半用複數形。

⓫branch：分公司、分支機構

⓬unrealistically：不切實際地

So sad, Barbara. My personal sales targets are unrealistically high next year.

好悲慘！Barbara。明年我個人銷售目標高到離譜！

⓭totally：完全地、全然地

Chloe, your explanations are totally unacceptable.

Chloe，我完全沒法接受妳的解釋。

NOTE

⑭ **Average Selling Price (ASP)**：平均售價

⑮ **contribution**：貢獻
成本會計上指銷貨收入扣除銷貨變動成本。

⑯ **tier 1 customers**：第一階客戶
指金字塔最高端、家數少、競爭少、高利潤型態的客戶群。

⑰ **guesstimation**：半猜測半估算的意思
是由「*guess*」和「*estimation*」連結的合成字。

⑱ **begin with**：從⋯開始

⑲ **category**：產品類別
Benny, I want know the sales figures of each product category.
Benny，我要知道每一類產品的銷售數字。

⑳ **model**：型號

㉑ **with full effort**：用盡全力、非常努力
Sam, I have put my full effort into helping you.
Sam，我已盡全力幫你忙了。

㉒ **in general**：大體來說

㉓ **look quite good**：看起來還不錯
Evan, your report looks quite good.
Evan，你的報告看起來不錯喔！

NOTE

㉔scare me：嚇我

Shoot, you're scaring me to death, John.

哇塞！John，你嚇得我半死啦！

㉕up by 25%：提高、增加**25%**

Good news, Nick. Our revenues last month were up by 25%.

好消息 Nick，我們上個月營收成長 25%。

㉖capacity utilization：產能使用率

㉗workable：可行的、可以安排的

Frank, please review my proposal and confirm if workable.

Frank，請你看看我的提議並確認是否可行。

㉘to our expectation：達到我們預期、符合我們的預期

Very sorry, Ryan. Your report doesn't come up to our expectation.

抱歉 Ryan，你的報告不符我們預期。

課文重點② Summary 2

Gaining agreement on the annual sales objectives are always difficult to achieve in the real business world. Very often, it becomes a <u>tug of war</u> between the boss in headquarters and sales managers in branch offices. <u>Consequently</u>, it is an extremely <u>time-consuming</u> and <u>tiring</u> task for the entire team. <u>Nevertheless</u>, it is of <u>vital</u> importance that <u>consensus</u> is reached <u>through</u> sufficient communications and negotiations. If there is any <u>discrepancy</u>, <u>apart from</u> <u>identifying</u> the causes, it is essential to work out a solution together. It would then become the <u>cornerstone</u> of the marketing/sales strategy for the year to come. The sales objectives will also be used for <u>KPI</u> and <u>PA</u> purposes within a business unit.

對所有業務單位或業務人員來說，每次新年度業務目標都高到不合理，完成這項不可能的任務就成了業務的宿命。因此制定年度銷售目標，就成為總公司業務總監與各分公司業務經理之間的拔河比賽，是一項既費時又吃重的工作。雙方唯有透過充分溝通協調才能達成共識。過程中歧見在所難免，除了找出問題點之

外，更重要的是雙方能想出解決方案。這解決方案，就成為公司來年行銷業務策略藍圖。而銷售目標也成為公司內部績效評核（PA）與衡量關鍵績效指標的一項重要指標。

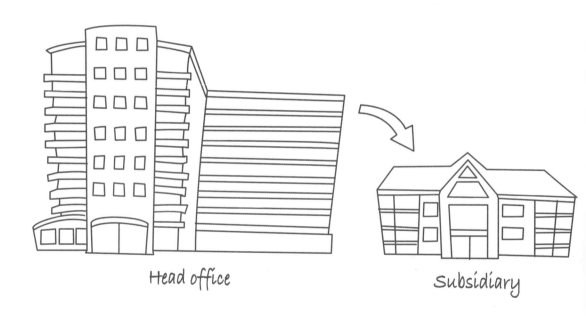

Head office   Subsidiary

總公司的期待：tug of war 🔘2-2

:**VP Global Sales, RL Precision (U.S.A.)**：全球業務
Nick 總監，美國

:**Senior Sales Manager, RL Asia (Taiwan)**：資深業
Paul 務經理，臺灣

:Hi Paul, good morning. I just saw the <u>spreadsheet</u> of your an-
Nick nual budget for <u>the coming year</u>. Before I have a chance to
review it <u>in detail</u>, we need to talk seriously about the <u>overall</u>
<u>sales objectives</u> of RL Asia. They are lower than the <u>guide-</u>
<u>lines</u> I <u>distributed</u> to you on the <u>con-call</u> <u>the other day</u>.

嗨 Paul，早安。我剛才看到你明年的預算試算表了。在我有機
會去看細項之前，我們得好好談談 RL Asia 的整體銷售目標。
你們編的銷售目標，要比我前幾天在視訊會議時傳給你們的參
考數字來得低。

Dr. Lee 解析

顯然在對話之前，Nick 已透過遠端視訊會議或電話會議，定
出明年 RL 各據點的銷售目標。然而在收到 RL Asia Paul 所提
交的年度預算後，發現所顯現的目標數字，顯然和原先 Nick
的期望數字有差距，特別打電話來質詢。

Paul：Good morning, Nick. Yes, we did <u>run into</u> some problems with some of the numbers I received from you. Please let me get all the data ready first and <u>I'll get back to you in a minute</u>.

早安 Nick。對，在我們用你的目標數字編預算時，確實碰到了一些問題。請先讓我把數據準備好，過一會兒回來找你。

Dr. Lee 解析

Paul 也不諱言表示，要達成 Nick 所期望的目標有困難。會立即準備好所有數據和 Nick 討論。

Nick：OK, Paul, <u>take your time</u>. I'll be in my office all day today.

好，不急慢慢來，Paul。我今天整天都會在辦公室。

Dr. Lee 解析

對老闆來說，手下業務達標與否，永遠都是大事一件。

Paul：Hi Nick, we can start now. Firstly let me explain how we <u>came up with</u> these numbers. The main reason for <u>failing to meet your expectation</u> is that most of our major customers will face a sales <u>downturn</u> next year.

嗨 Nick，現在可以開始了。首先，讓我說明那些數字是怎麼來的。之所以沒能達到你的期望，最主要是因為我們許多大客戶明年銷售預估也下滑。

Dr. Lee 解析

> Paul 開門見山就表示，來年因手中幾家大客戶出貨展望不佳，業績將大受影響。

😊 : Well, it seems you make a good point but I'm sorry it isn't
Nick
acceptable. Bear in mind we have a set of tough objectives to
achieve next year for our entire BU. It's reasonable that each
office shares a heavier load.

聽起來你們似乎有理，不過很抱歉，我無法接受這樣說法。請
記住，明年我們整個事業體的銷售目標，都將會是困難重重。
所以每個據點多分擔些責任很合理。

Dr. Lee 解析

> 老闆不是幹假的，哪會輕易採信這種說法？況且集團也要求
> Nick 明年業績得大幅成長，自然會向下要求各據點，同時多
> 分攤業績壓力。

😊 : Nick, Apart from the reason I just mentioned, our pricing
Paul
strategy also puts us in an unfavorable position. Since we are
going to increase our MSP and ASP starting Q1 next year, I
would foresee further decrease in sales by then.

Nick，除了剛剛我提的原因外，我們的價格策略也不利我們
在市場上競爭。由於我們從明年第一季開始又要調升我們的
MSP 與 ASP，我可預見到時訂單會減少。

Dr. Lee 解析

> Paul 是老鳥了，又提出另一理由，就是公司明年還打算漲價。已經預見大客戶會流失大半，還得漲價？這哪成啊？

Nick : Paul, let me give you a complete picture of RL's divisional objectives. It will help you understand your position in the entire division. I just saw RL Asia's overall sales growth for the coming year to be 11% only. You must realize that the entire RL Division is expected to achieve an 18% sales growth next year, a much more aggressive goal.

我先告訴你整個 RL 事業體的目標情況，來幫你了解 RL Asia 的地位。我剛才看到 RL Asia 明年的銷售成長率只有 11%；但你得了解，整個 RL 事業體明年的營收成長目標高達 18%。那是一個超困難的目標。

Dr. Lee 解析

> 溝通雙方都需相互尊重就事論事，表明立場說明實情。Nick 還是耐心說明，先讓 Paul 了解他自己的壓力有多大。也一併告知事業體整體目標，好讓 Paul 明白，其實 RL Asia 來年的困境，已經被考慮進去了。

Paul : I got it, but how about RL divisional MSP/ASP objective? Will it be an across-the-board increase? All our customers said that 10% increase is way too high to accept.

我知道了。不過 RL 事業體的 MSP/ASP 目標如何呢？會全面

調高嗎？每家客人都說上漲 10% 實在太高，無法接受。

Dr. Lee 解析

不妨再強調主要問題與可能後果。Paul 依然擔心來年漲價可能帶來的衝擊，表示客戶不會接受。

😊 : Well, I'm <u>determined</u> to <u>implement</u> the MSP/ASP increase
Nick starting Jan. 1. And it will definitely be executed across the board with very few <u>exceptions, if any</u>. You will be receiving the new <u>price matrix</u> for both MSP and ASP <u>in a day or two</u>.

嗯，我是鐵了心，一定要在明年元月一日開始實施 MSP/ASP 調升。而且一定是全面性漲價，幾乎沒有例外。你會在一兩天內收到新的 MSP 和 ASP 的價格矩陣表。

Dr. Lee 解析

策略是否奏效，堅持是關鍵，沒得商量。老闆吃了秤砣鐵了心，決心要漲價，而且是全面漲，所有客戶所有品項都得漲。連新的價格表都已準備好了。

😊 : <u>For sure</u> it will be very tough for us, with Japan and Taiwan
Paul <u>in particular</u>. We are facing a <u>structural change</u> in the customer base of these two important markets. Many of our <u>tier 3 customers</u> will either move their manufacturing to China or change their current business model into a <u>buy-and-resell</u> one. Either will lead to a decrease in demand for our products.

漲價對我們來說,特別是日本和臺灣,真的很吃力。在這兩大市場裡,我們都面臨著客戶群結構的改變,許多第三階的客戶,不是遷廠至中國,就是改變現有營運模式,只做轉賣生意了。這都會導致訂單減少。

Dr. Lee 解析

有必要就得舉例說明,讓主管理解重要細節。Paul 還是想據理力爭,點出真正問題所在。臺灣與日本 OEM 大廠西遷或停產,衝擊太大。

Nick : I understand it and that's why we would only expect a <u>mild</u> sales growth from you next year. Paul, we've talked about this a few times before and I'm confident that your team will be able to make it <u>eventually</u>.

我了解,所以我對 RL Asia 明年業績,只期望能有微幅成長。Paul,對於這議題,我們先前已經談過幾次了。我相信到頭來,你的團隊還是能辦到的。

Dr. Lee 解析

即使充分溝通,雙方也不見得就能有共識,這很正常。Nick 表示已經有考慮這些變化了,並且以打氣鼓勵方式希望 Paul 勉為其難。

Paul: We'll <u>do everything possible</u> to perform, no doubt about it. Developing new business will be our number one task since we will lose <u>a big chunk of</u> tier 3 sales. Actually we have already started to attack new markets such as machine builders for automation and industrial control industries. Hopefully we'll start to get new business by the end of Q1 next year.

沒問題，我們會盡全力完成。由於我們會丟掉一大塊第三階客戶的生意，所以開發新市場將會是我們團隊的首要工作。其實，我們已經開始打入某些新市場了，例如自動化和工業控制機器製造商這兩個區塊。我們希望到明年第一季末，可以開始拿到一些新訂單。

Dr. Lee 解析

大方向既然已定，下屬就得讓老闆信任自己。Paul 則表示，已經著手開發新市場與新客戶，來填補大客戶流失的訂單缺口。提出行動方案永遠是最好的答覆。

Nick: That's great. I'm glad to know you guys <u>took action</u> already. And I believe you'll be able to achieve the target for new customers as well as new business. We always need new business. I realize how difficult it is to <u>fill up</u> the hole caused by the <u>lost business</u> from those tier 3 customers.

太好了，很高興你們已經有動作。相信你們團隊無論是在開發新客戶，或是新生意方面，都能達標的。我們永遠都需要有新生意，我了解要填補失去第三階客戶的定單大洞會有多困難。

Dr. Lee 解析

老闆還是得適時給予鼓勵，但也不斷提醒下屬，得想盡一切辦法達成目標。

Paul

: Yes, you're right. The hole is too big to fill with new business alone. We'll have to get a lot more support from our existing accounts, especially from those major tier 2 customers. By <u>expanding</u> our share in the tier 2 market, we will also <u>improve</u> our ASP significantly.

沒錯，那個缺口太大了，是沒法單靠新訂單就能補起來的。我們還是得從其他現有客戶，尤其是大型的第二階客戶那裡，拿到更多生意才行。另外，提高我們在第二階客戶的市占率，也能大大改善我們的 ASP。

Dr. Lee 解析

Paul 顯然未雨綢繆已有所準備，並提出現有第二類客戶的重要性。

Nick

: Now we need to review the objectives of RL Asia's individual markets. Let's begin with Japan. I think 10% growth is too low. Although you will lose the support from a couple of OEM customers, I need you to <u>gear up</u> faster and come up with a 15% growth. Meanwhile, you'll find in the new price matrix that both MSP and ASP will be up by 10%.

現在，我們得來看看 RL Asia 個別市場的銷售目標了。先從日

本開始，我認為 10% 成長率太低。雖然你們會丟掉幾家 OEM 客戶的訂單，我還是希望你們加把勁，做到 15%。另外，從新的價格表裡，你們可以看到日本的 MSP 和 ASP 都調漲了 10%。

Dr. Lee 解析

> 看完整體情況，Nick 準備由日本開始，逐一檢視單一市場。

Paul : We will <u>expedite</u> the <u>ongoing ODM projects</u> to <u>make up</u> the <u>shortfall</u> <u>on one hand</u> and improve the ASP <u>on the other</u>. <u>Meanwhile</u>, we're working closely with our master distributor for more business. I'll be visiting them next week and will discuss with Mr. Kushida in detail. Basically, I'm more comfortable with Japan than with Taiwan, in terms of <u>business prospects</u> for next year.

我們一方面加快進行中的 ODM 專案，以便彌補訂單的減少。另一方面，也能藉此拉高 ASP。同時，我們正和代理商更密切合作增加生意量。我下週將去拜訪他們，並且會和 Kushida 社長仔細討論。展望明年，相對臺灣，我對日本市場還比較有信心。

Dr. Lee 解析

> Paul 還是充分顯出老經驗業務的功力，直接提出解決方案：加速現有 ODM 結案，以及向代理商施加壓力。

Nick : That's good. I'm a bit surprised to find you are <u>pessimistic</u> about the business in Taiwan. You guys have been doing so well in recent years. I'd like to hear more from you and hopefully I can help you find a solution. Please bear in mind that your problem is my problem, too.

很好啊！我倒是很訝異你對臺灣市場這麼悲觀，這麼多年來，你們表現一直很好。我想多聽聽你的想法，希望能幫你找到解決辦法。記住，你的問題就是我的問題。

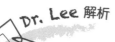

Dr. Lee 解析

老闆對於主力市場自然特別關心，也比較願意出力協助。Paul 對於自家後院臺灣市場的不樂觀，引起 Nick 高度關切，並表示將全力支援。

Paul : Thanks very much. It is tougher than I've expected. We have been constantly <u>exchanging dialogues</u> with all the big OEM customers <u>concerning</u> their future <u>commitments</u>. None of them were <u>optimistic</u> and decided to move their purchasing to their main manufacturing site in China. Unfortunately, the said tier 3 business <u>accounted for</u> more than 45% of our total Taiwan revenue.

謝謝！臺灣的問題比我預期的還困難。針對未來的業務展望，我們一直不斷的和所有大型 OEM 客戶保持對話，但是他們全都不樂觀。而且已經將採購移到中國廠了。很不幸的，這些第三階客戶的總需求量，就占掉臺灣總營收的 45%。

Dr. Lee 解析

產業結構變化導致的客戶流失也是無奈，Paul 表示大勢難以挽回。第三階 OEM 客戶所占業績比重太高，這是令 Paul 頭疼的大問題。

Nick : Now I see why you're <u>concerned</u> so much about your objectives as Taiwan has been the <u>mainstay</u> of entire RL Asia. If Taiwan runs into trouble, RL Asia will definitely be in deep trouble. I think we should start <u>doing something about this right away</u>.

現在我能了解你為何會這麼擔心 RL Asia 的銷售目標了。因為臺灣一直是 RL Asia 裡最重要的區塊，一旦臺灣遇上麻煩，RL Asia 絕對跟著遭殃。我認為我們得快點想出對策才行。

Dr. Lee 解析

老闆 Nick 表示理解嚴重性，並表示應該採取行動了。

Paul : Certainly, and I'll send my <u>proposition</u> to you very soon for further discussion.

那當然。我會很快把建議報告傳給你，好進一步和你討論。

Dr. Lee 解析

Paul 已準備好後續動作，務必將衝擊減至最小。

Nick: That's great. Now let's move on to Korea. I can see Korea is pretty much on the right track, keeping up with our objective guidelines. The figures look good, a 20% increase in sales value and a 10% increase in ASP. They just look good. But Paul, you need to develop more new customers.

太好了。我們來看看韓國吧！看得出來，韓國還不錯，都能達成 20% 成長率和 10% ASP 調漲的目標，看來真不錯。不過 Paul，你們得多開發些新客戶。

Dr. Lee 解析

韓國似乎還 OK，Nick 還是提醒得開發新客戶。

Paul: Yes, you're right. The Korean market is fairly small in size however with good potential to grow. In fact, to penetrate into Korea is even tougher than into Japan. It also takes a longer time for us to develop to a desired level. We've been working with several potential customers for some time. We're confident some of them will start doing business with us soon.

對，正是如此。韓國市場比較小，不過還是有很好的成長潛力。實際上，要打入韓國市場，甚至比打入日本還困難。而且還得花更長時間，才能把韓國市場做出一些名堂。我們已經努力在一些潛力客戶身上下工夫。相信過不久，就會有他們的生意了。

Dr. Lee 解析

> 韓國難打，甚至比日本還封閉還難打入。趁檢討會提出問題，
> 是讓主管快速了解重點的最佳方法。

Nick：Job <u>very well done</u> and I'm glad to hear that. Now let's go down to the Southeast Asia market. It is a fairly <u>fragmented</u> region. I learned there are a few bigger markets and several small ones. Overall, I accept your propositions of 20% growth in total sales and 10% increase in ASP.

做得很好，聽你這麼說我很高興。現在來看看東南亞市場，這區域還蠻零散的。據我了解，有幾個較大的市場，和其他幾個小市場。整體來說，我接受你提案的 20% 成長率和 10% 的 ASP 調漲目標。

Dr. Lee 解析

> 東南亞呈現多國多樣化局面，大小市場並存。

Paul：Among these 6 countries, Malaysia and Thailand belong to class A market <u>while the rest are class B.</u> We'll be more focusing on class A countries in the coming year. We are expecting to <u>overtake</u> HVM and become number one supplier in the region. Expanding existing distributors of class A countries will be our growth strategy.

在 6 個國家中，馬來西亞和泰國屬於 A 級市場，其他都是 B 級。明年我們會集中火力在 A 級市場，希望能追過 HVM 而在東南

亞稱霸。基本上，我們的成長策略就是擴大和這兩家總代理的生意量。

Dr. Lee 解析

> 區隔與標定顯得格外重要，Paul 採用 80/20 原理，掌握重點，企圖稱霸。能明確說出目標與方法最重要。

Nick: Now, the two countries in the southern hemisphere, New Zealand and Australia. It seems to me you are struggling in both countries. The proposed 10% sales growth for both countries is too low. I'm going to revise it to 15% instead. The increase of ASP will still be 10%.

現在來看看南半球的紐西蘭和澳洲這二個國家。看起來，你們在這裡陷入苦戰。你提的 10% 成長率太低了，我要把它改成 15%，ASP 則維持原案調漲 10%。

Dr. Lee 解析

> Nick 不滿意 Paul 對紐、澳這兩個南半球市場的慵懶表現。

Paul: Actually, we're facing a serious problem in the region. That is, insufficient application support. More and more end customers have been asking for technical or application support. Our master distributors are rather weak in this regard. We'll be working closely with our distributors with the help of our advanced CRM system. It enables our FAE to spend more

time with their technical team online to solve the <u>day-to-day</u>
technical problems. We really hope <u>by doing so</u> things will
<u>get better and better</u>.

實際上，我們在這地區面臨一個嚴重問題，就是應用支援不足。
越來越多終端客戶要求我們提供技術和應用支援，而我們的總
代理在這方面又很弱。未來我們要和他們密切合作，利用公司
先進的 CRM 系統，讓我們應用工程師提供線上服務，協助客
戶技術團隊解決日常的技術問題。希望這樣能逐漸改善技術支
援不足的問題。

Dr. Lee 解析

業績不佳，主事者必須清楚明白癥結所在，並擬定好解決之
道。Paul 指出，公司在應用工程支援上的不足，影響業務推展。
Paul 團隊未來將依賴 CRM 系統，改善這問題。

Nick : Very good, Paul. We've covered all the countries under your
jurisdiction. I'm quite <u>comfortable</u> with the way you are lead-
ing your team. Should you need any help, <u>give me a buzz</u> any
time, OK?

幹得好，Paul。我們談完了你的轄區，對於你帶業務團隊的方
式，我很放心。如果你還需要什麼，儘管來找我，好嗎？

Dr. Lee 解析

首輪討論結束，可能還得再經過幾次來回的溝通協調，最後銷售目標才能定案。

Paul：I'll surely do it. Thanks.
沒問題。謝謝。

NOTE

❶tug of war：拔河
指雙方為了年度目標高低與合理性的角力。

❷Consequently：因此、所以
Consequently, Bobby was asked to leave.
因此，Bobby 被解雇了。

❸time-consuming：耗時的
I hate to do this as it is so time-consuming.
我厭惡做這件事，太耗時間了！

❹tiring：令人疲倦的、累人的
Being stuck at the airport for whatever the reason can be very tiring.
無論是什麼原因，被困在機場都是很累人的。

NOTE

⑤ nevertheless：然而、但是

Yes, we're all tired. Nevertheless, we still have to get this done in time.

沒錯我們都很累，然而我們還是得及時把這做完。

⑥ vital：極端重要的、生死攸關的

Intrinsically safe systems are vital in a hazardous working environment.

本質安全系統在危險工作環境內是非常重要的。

⑦ consensus：共識

Regarding possible solutions, we did reach a consensus.

關於可能的解決方案，我們倒是達成了共識。

⑧ through：經由、藉由

⑨ discrepancy：差異、落差

Nick wants us to explain the discrepancies in details.

Nick 要我們詳細說明落差由何而來。

⑩ apart from：除了…之外

Apart from working on the sales budget, we also have to do an expenditure budget.

除了做銷售預算，我們還得做支出預算。

⑪ identify：識別、認出

You have to identify yourself before entering the lab.

你必須表明身份後才能進入實驗室。

NOTE

⑫**cornerstones**：基石

⑬**KPI**：關鍵績效指標、重要績效指標

是 Key Performance Indicators 的縮寫。

Most product marketing people are evaluated by a set of KPIs including the number of qualified sales leads, sales lead conversion, ROI of marketing investment, pricing effectiveness, new product development effectiveness, and channel management effectiveness.

多數產品行銷人員的關鍵績效指標包括：有效銷售線索數目、銷售線索轉換率、行銷投資報酬率、定價成效、新產品開發成效、以及通路管理成效。

⑭**PA**：績效評核

Performance Appraisal 的縮寫。

⑮**spreadsheet**：試算表

這裡是指自訂的銷售目標試算表。

⑯**the coming year**：來年、下一年

⑰**in detail**：仔細、詳細

Hank, please explain the variances in detail.

Hank，請你詳細解釋那些差異。

⑱**overall sales objectives**：整體業務目標

NOTE

⑲ **guideline**：行動準則、行動方針
Hey guys, please follow the guidelines I sent to you earlier for your forecasts.
各位，請按照我稍早傳給你們的準則做預估。

⑳ **distribute**：分發、分給
Ella, make sure to distribute the meeting minutes to everybody who attended the meeting.
Ella，務必將會議記錄分發給每位出席開會的人。

㉑ **con-call**：多方電話會議
conference call 的縮寫。

㉒ **the other day**：前幾天、前些日子

㉓ **run into**：遇上、碰到
Sharon, call me if you run into any trouble on the road.
Sharon，出差途中若碰上任何麻煩，儘管打電話給我。

㉔ **I'll get back to you in a minute**：我等一下回你

㉕ **take your time**：不急、慢慢來

㉖ **come up with**：提出、想出
After discussing for 4 hours, the marketing team came up with an 11-page proposal.
經過 4 小時討論，行銷團隊提出一份 11 頁的提案。

NOTE

27 fail to：無法、沒能

Natalie, failing to keep the promises that you made to your customers is absolutely a no-no as a salesperson.

Natalie，無法信守妳對客戶的承諾，是當業務的一大禁忌。

28 meet your expectation：達到你的期望

29 downturn：下滑、衰退

Noah is under tremendous pressure because of the recent sales downturn.

最近的業務衰退帶給 Noah 極大的壓力。

30 it seems：好像、似乎

James, it seems that something's on your mind.

James，你似乎有心事。

31 make a good point：說得有道理

Dan, I guess you've made a good point.

Dan，我認為你說得有道理。

32 bear in mind：記住、牢記

Victoria, bear in mind installing a new website is our number one priority next year.

Victoria，請牢記，架設一個全新網站是我們明年最優先的工作。

33 BU：事業體、營運單位

Business Unit 的縮寫。

NOTE

㉞ load：負荷、負重、這裡指責任

㉟ unfavorable position：不利的地位或情勢

Nick, the delay of OCXO project has put us in an unfavorable position competing with AXC.

Nick，OCXO 專案延誤，不利我們和 AXC 的競爭。

㊱ foresee：預見

Bob, we can foresee that a price war is coming.

Bob，我們可以預見一場即將到來的價格戰。

㊲ complete picture：整體狀況

㊳ realize：明白、了解、知道

Evan, I hope you realize what I'm expecting you to achieve.

Evan，我希望你了解我對你的期望。

㊴ aggressive：具有野心的

指大膽的、衝勁十足的。

Susan, I want you to become more aggressive in getting sales results.

Susan，我要妳更積極更大膽地去拿訂單。

㊵ I got it：我明白了、我知道了、我記下來了

㊶ across-the-board：全面性的

Headquarters just announced an across-the-board price hike.

總公司剛剛宣布了一項全面性漲價。

NOTE

㊷way too high：太高了、高過頭了、高得離譜了

Lisa, the quote we received from Jamie.com for our new website is way too high.

Lisa，Jamie.com 剛報給我們的新網站製作價格高得太離譜了。

㊸determined：下定決心的、有決心的

Guys, I'm determined to implement the price increase regardless of the resistance from the customers.

各位，儘管有來自客戶的阻力，我還是下定決心要實施漲價。

㊹implement：實施、執行

㊺exception：例外

There are always exceptions.

一定會有例外情況的。

㊻if any：如果還有的話

Mike, I'm afraid we have little hope, if any, to win GL's server order this year.

Mike，今年我們拿到 GL 伺服器訂單的機會，即便有恐怕也非常渺茫了。

㊼price matrix：價格矩陣表

指詳細價格表。

㊽in a day or two：一、二天之內，或泛指幾天之內

NOTE

㊾ **for sure**：確定、一定

Emma, there will be a price hike, for sure.

Emma，漲價一定會實施。

㊿ **in particular**：特別是

也可說 particularly。

Japan and Taiwan in particular were hurt badly by the price increase.

特別是日本和臺灣，受這次漲價傷害最大。

(51) **structural change**：結構上的改變

Our main customer base went through a structural change last year.

我們主要客戶群經過了結構上改變。

(52) **tier 3 customers**：第三階客戶

指生意量特大但利潤低，金字塔底層的大型客戶。

(53) **buy-and-resell**：純買賣，買來轉售的生意型態

(54) **mild**：溫和的，不太高的

We enjoyed a mild growth from the Australian market last year.

去年我們在澳洲市場稍有成長。

(55) **eventually**：終究、到最後

NOTE

56 do everything possible：盡一切可能

possible 要放在 everything 之後。

Denise, we'll do everything possible to pull in delivery for you.

Denise，我們會盡一切可能提前交貨給你們。

57 a big chunk of：一大塊，很多的、很大的

We won back a big chunk of Dax's server business from AXC by offering VMI hub service.

藉由提供 VMI 倉服務，我們從 AXC 手中奪回一大塊 Dax 伺服器的生意。

58 take action：採取行動，有動作

We were forced to take action and fight back.

我們被迫採取行動回擊。

59 fill up：填滿、補滿

60 lost business：失去、失掉的生意（訂單）

Morris, it's very hard for us to fill up the huge amount of lost business that occurred last quarter.

Morris，要彌補上季丟掉的大單實在非常困難。

61 expand：擴大、加大

62 improve：改善、改進

NOTE

(63) **gear up**：上檔

表示加緊腳步、加速。

OK guys, we need to gear up and get more orders.

各位，我們得加緊腳步多接單啊！

(64) **expedite**：加快、加速

Cindy, we're still waiting for your monthly statistics. Please expedite.

Cindy，我們都還在等你的月統計數字，快點呀！

(65) **ongoing ODM projects**：正在進行的**ODM**專案

ongoing 進行中的。

(66) **make up**：補償、補足

Allison, we'll have to gear up and make up the shortfall out of the two unexpected non-working days.

Allison，由於意外的兩天假，我們得加緊腳步，補起不足的訂單。

(67) **shortfall**：短少、不足

(68) **on one hand…on the other**：一方面…另一方面

We industrial marketing people are responsible for strengthening customer relationships on one hand and laying down a comprehensive product roadmap on the other.

我們工業行銷人員一方面得負責強化客戶關係，另一方面還得負責制定出完整的產品藍圖。

NOTE

69 **meanwhile**：同時、在此期間

也可說 in the mean time。

70 **business prospect**：對…生意（訂單）的展望

Lily, business prospect for the next 12 months is not good.

Lily，未來 12 個月的產業展望並不好。

71 **pessimistic**：悲觀、不看好

72 **exchange dialogue**：對話、溝通、交換意見

To some industries, exchanging dialogues among competing firms can be extremely sensitive.

對某些產業來說，競爭廠家之間進行對話是一件極端敏感的事情。

73 **concerning**：關於

74 **commitment**：承諾，意指訂單、生意的承諾

75 **optimistic**：樂觀的、看好的。

反義字：pessimistic 悲觀的。

76 **account for**：佔了（多少比例、比重）

Taiwan sales accounted for more than 40% of our total Asia sales last year.

去年臺灣的營收占了我們亞洲總營收四成以上。

NOTE

⑦ concern：擔心、煩惱、顧慮、關心

Mason, Tim and I are concerned about our relationships with Raytheon.

Mason，Tim 和我很擔心我們和 Raytheon 的關係。

⑱ mainstay：支柱、最重要的支撐

Titanium alloy and stainless alloy are still the mainstays of our company.

鈦合金和不鏽鋼合金依舊是我們公司的主力產品。

⑲ do something about this：（針對事情或問題）想點辦法解決或拿出作為

Under such circumstances, we have to do something about it quickly.

在這種情況下，我們得迅速想出解決辦法。

⑳ right away：立即、馬上

㉑ proposition：建議報告、提議書

也可用 proposal。

㉒ on the right track：在正確的道路上

意指做得很對、很正常。

Three months after the system change, we're finally back on the right track.

在系統轉換三個月之後，我們終於又回到正軌上了。

NOTE

83 keep up with：保持、跟得上，意指與目標同步

We are able to keep up with the sales target, thanks to the efforts from each team member.

由於每位團隊成員的努力，我們還能夠跟得上業績目標。

84 good potential：很有潛力、有好潛力

Matt is a smart kid with good potential.

Matt 是一位有潛力的年輕小夥子。

85 penetrate into：滲透進

指打入（市場）。

86 desired：希望的、期望的

Jeremy, it might not be a desired result for you.

Jeremy，那可能不是你所期望的結果。

87 confident：有信心

We're confident in penetrating into the New Zealand market.

我們有信心打入紐西蘭市場。

88 job very well done：工作或事情做得很好

89 fragmented：支離破碎的，這裡指大小市場參雜

NOTE

⑨⓪ while the rest are class B：而其餘的（市場）屬B級

在此，while 這連接詞有「而」或「當」的意思，但 while 後所指的與 while 前所指的，是屬於不相等或相反的二類事物。

John seems to be happy, while the others were worrying about the heavy rain.

John 似乎還很開心，而其他人都在擔心這場大雨。

⑨① overtake：超越、超過

也可說 surpass。超車也可用 overtake。

Bosco, for sure we'll overtake AXC in TCXO sales next year.

Bosco，明年我們 TCXO 營收絕對會超過 AXC。

⑨② southern hemisphere：南半球

⑨③ struggle：掙扎，陷入困境

UMS has been struggling with the 28nm production and yield as well.

UMS 在 28 奈米製程與良率上一直陷入苦戰。

⑨④ revise：修正、修改

Elizabeth, you need to revise your Q2 forecast according to the guidelines we worked out yesterday.

Elizabeth，妳得根據我們昨天提出的原則修正妳的 Q2 預估。

NOTE

⑨⑤instead：使用在句尾有「而是」的意思

Jason, we didn't recommend model 120 to UTE. We proposed model 220 instead.

Jason，我們並沒推薦 UTE 用型號 120，而是建議他們用型號 220。

⑨⑥insufficient：不足的、不夠的

Insufficient technical support is our fatal weakness.

技術支援不足是我們的致命傷。

⑨⑦rather：這裡指「相當」的意思

rather weak 相當弱。

⑨⑧advanced：先進的、進步的

We acquired a more advanced CNC machine from a German company.

我們向一家德國廠商買了一臺更先進的 CNC。

⑨⑨FAE：應用工程師

Field Application Engineer 的縮寫。

⑩⑩day-to-day：日常的、平常的

⑩①by doing so：藉由如此的作為或行動

Susan, by doing so, I'm sure you'll get better and better.

Susan，如此一來，妳的表現絕對會越來越好。

NOTE

102 **get better and better**：變得越來越好

103 **comfortable**：安心、舒適、自在

Fiona, please make yourself comfortable.

Fiona，請別拘束放輕鬆些。

104 **give me a buzz**：打電話給我（多為口語使用）

Jeffrey, give me a buzz once you've landed at Taipei airport.

Jeffrey，一旦班機降落臺北機場，就打電話給我。

課文重點① **Summary 1**

Market segmentation is one of the most important tasks before any marketing strategy is laid out. Industrial marketers tend to divide the market into meaningful segments based on application, business type or company size. It serves as a map for the company to decide the optimal product/market mix to pursue. It also helps salespeople allocate their limited resource more effectively on a day-to-day basis.

許多工業產品橫跨多種產業，看似存在許多商機。然而公司資源有限，勢必得明確找出最適當的「產品／市場」組合，將資源做最有效運用。市場區隔就成為制定行銷策略前最重要的工作之一。工業行銷人員常依據應用場合、經營型態、或規模大小，將市場分割成若干小區塊。市場區隔不但是行銷人員最重要的工作之一，同時也能幫助業務人員有效規劃與執行日常銷售工作。

市場區隔：segmentation 3-1

> **Jenny**：**Senior Purchaser, Moore Technology (Singapore)**：資深採購，新加坡
>
> **Steve**：**Sales VP, Canter Tech (Taiwan)**：業務副總，臺灣
> **Video conference** 視訊會議

Jenny：Hi Steve. Thanks very much for sending me the PowerPoint materials about your company. It was <u>encouraging</u> to know that there might be plenty of business opportunities between our two companies. <u>Specifically</u>, I'd like to know more about the product/market analysis you mentioned. I'm sorry I forgot the term you used.

嗨 Steve，謝謝你提供你們公司的簡報。我很興奮從裡面發現了很多可能的商機。我特別想多了解你們的產品／市場組合分析，抱歉我忘了你們是用哪個名詞。

Steve：Oh, that's <u>STP</u>, an important part of our marketing strategy. I'm glad you found it useful. Now you may go to slide 12 and I'll give you a detailed explanation.

噢，那是 STP。是我們行銷策略很重要的一部份。很高興你覺得這部份對你有幫助，現在可以來看第 12 頁投影片，我仔細說明給你聽。

Jenny：Oh, <u>here it is</u>. When I first saw this, I was <u>confused</u> because it looked quite <u>complicated</u>.

嗯，找到了。那天我第一次瞄到這部份時感到有些不明白，因為內容看起來太複雜了。

Steve
: Let's start with the "S" segmentation. Basically we segment the entire market based on applications. You can see these are the major applications of our frequency control components. They are communications, consumer electronics, IT products, and automotive.

當然可以。我們就從 "S" 市場區隔開始吧。基本上，我們是以應用來區隔市場。妳可看到這些都是頻率控制元件的重要應用，就是通訊、消費性電子、資訊產品、以及車用電子裝置。

Jenny
: So we are in the consumer electronics segment, is that right?

所以說，我們是在消費性電子這區塊，對吧？

Steve
: Exactly. And it can be further divided into some smaller segments such as PC, NB, tablets, smartphones, digital cameras, video game consoles, and so on.

正確。而且這區塊還能進一步被分割成更小的區塊，像是桌機、筆電、平板、智慧型手機、數位相機、遊戲主機等等。

Jenny
: Yeah, I can see we are in a number of these segments, but what's our position anyway?

沒錯，可以看出我們分布在幾個區塊裡。可是，我們的份量到底如何呢？

Steve
: It is easy to tell. Here's the table showing the rankings by sales amount of our major customers. You're our number five customer. For your information, we have more than 200 customers.

由這張按銷售金額排序的統計圖表，很容易能看出來貴公司是本公司第五大客戶。一個數字提供你參考：我們共有超過 200

家客戶。

Jenny：I believe we are also fairly prominent in your IT segment, aren't we?

我相信，在 IT 這塊我們也很突出，不是嗎？

Steve：Yes, you're right. Now you should know how important you are to us.

沒錯。現在妳該明白貴公司對我們有多麼重要了吧！

NOTE

❶market segmentation：市場區隔

❷lay out：提出（計畫）

The product development plan for 240DSS has been laid out after numerous cross-functional meetings.

經過無數次跨部門會議後，240DSS 的產品開發案細項計畫總算完成。

❸business type：經營型態

❹optimal：最佳的、最適宜的

Hank, I guess that the optimal solution to this problem is to achieve a balance between the revenues and the margins.

Hank，我認為解決這問題的最好方法是在營收與毛利之間取得平衡。

❺product/market mix：產品／市場組合

NOTE

⑥ **pursue**：追求

As the market leader, we are determined to pursue higher profitability.

做為市場龍頭老大，我們決心追求更高獲利率。

⑦ **encouraging**：令人鼓舞的、令人興奮的

⑧ **specifically**：特別地、特定地

⑨ **STP**：市場區隔、目標鎖定、產品定位

Segmentation, Targeting, Positioning 的縮寫。

⑩ **here it is**：找到了、在這裡、給你的意思

多用於口語。

⑪ **confuse**：迷惑、弄亂

⑫ **complicated**：複雜

⑬ **applications**：應用、應用場合

⑭ **communications, consumer electronics, IT products, and automotive**：通訊、消費性電子產品、資訊產品、與車用裝置

⑮ **PC, NB, tablets, smartphones, digital cameras, video game consoles**：桌機、筆電、平板、智慧型手機、數位相機、遊戲主機

NOTE

⑯**a number of**：許多、有些、若干

A number of our colleagues came from overseas.
我們同事當中不少來自海外。

⑰**it is easy to tell**：容易看出、容易辨認

⑱**rankings by sales amount**：以銷售金額大小排序

注意介系詞用 by。

課文重點② Summary 2

It is <u>essential</u> for a B2B marketer or a B2B salesperson to know who the customers are and how important they are in order to <u>distribute</u> his or her limited <u>resources</u> more effectively. This is what the most profitable B2B firms do, and this is what makes them <u>excel</u>. For most industrial products, the industry or the total market can be divided into three <u>tiers</u>, namely Tier 1, Tier 2, and Tier 3. Very often, marketers do this based on application, business <u>scale</u>, <u>geographic region</u>, or profitability. Each tier can be further divided into smaller segments that may have a different <u>character or nature</u>. <u>By doing so</u>, salespeople may easily review and monitor the performance of their individual customers <u>systematically</u>. Together with other management tools such as the <u>80/20 principle</u>, segmentation helps both the managers and the salespeople plan and <u>execute</u> their day-to-day work in a more effective <u>manner</u>.

對所有 B2B 行銷或業務人員來說，一定得清楚了解客戶在哪裡、商機在哪裡、個別重要性如何，才能有效分配有限資源。企業獲利能力高低端賴業務團隊這種基本功是否紮實。工業廠家經常根據各種指標，如產品應用、規模大小、地理區域、或獲利高低，將產業市場分為三大區塊，即第一階 (Tier1)、第二階 (Tier 2)、與第三階 (Tier 3) 市場或客戶群。每塊區隔裡，可再細分為不同性質的小區塊，方便行銷及業務人員系統性追蹤、檢視目標客戶的業績進度。此外，業務人員也經常運用 80/20 法則，更有效地從事日常工作計畫與執行。

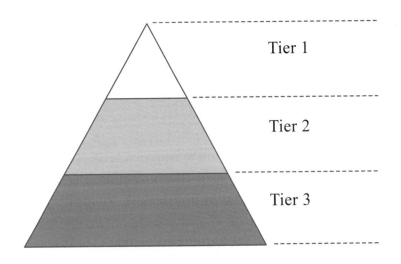

標定與定位：targeting & positioning 3-2

Allen ：**Marketing VP, distributor of VT Taiwan in Australia**：行銷副總，澳洲代理

Monica ：**Sales Manager, VT Taiwan**：業務經理，**VT**台灣

Video conference 視訊會議

Monica ：Hi Allen, this is Monica from VT Taiwan, how are you doing?

嗨 Allen，我是 VT Taiwan 的 Monica，你好嗎？

Monica 很自然的電話禮儀。

Allen ：Hello Monica, I'm doing great, thanks. How about yourself?

哈囉 Monica，謝謝，我很好。妳呢？

Allen 的回覆很有活力。

Monica ：Very busy, Allen. We need to continue the discussion we had last week regarding developing business in a number of new market segments in Australia.

Allen，我超忙的。我們得繼續上星期有關開發澳洲新生意的討論。

Monica 想要繼續前一星期有關開發新生意的討論。

: Oh yes, Monica, we'd better do it quickly as time is running short. I feel comfortable with your suggestion that we divide our business into three tiers, Tier 1, Tier 2, and Tier 3.

是的 Monica，時間不多了，我們得快點。我覺得妳的建議很好，將我們的業務分成三階：第一階、第二階、和第三階。

Allen 也覺得馬上要進入新年度了，的確應該加緊腳步。此時，Allen 也將前次 Monica 所建議的三分法提出來。

: Good, let's start from there. Please refer to slide number 5 in the file I sent to you earlier this morning. I suggest that we start with Tier 3 considering its huge business scale.

好，就從這裡開始好了。請參考上午稍早我傳過去的電子檔第五張投影片，由於第三階生意金額龐大，我建議就從這裡開始討論。

Dr. Lee 解析

由於第三階市場（Tier 3）生意規模最大，雙方就由首先討論。

Allen : We both realize that we didn't have the right weapons to attack the tier 3 market until now. As I said the other day, we are aiming at the food processing applications with our new SS, IP68 transducers and our DQ IP67 indicator. However, since all of these products are new to the market, we need to do a lot of marketing before talking to our customers.

你我都明白，我們一直到現在才開發出適合第三階市場的產品。我幾天前說過，我們要拿新開發成功的不鏽鋼 IP68 傳感器，和 IP67 DQ 顯示器瞄準食品加工應用區塊。不過因為才剛推出，在開始找客人談之前，我們得先有行銷動作才行。

Dr. Lee 解析

以往，VT 沒有合適的產品可用在食品加工業的高濕、高溫操作環境裡。因此，VT 在這規模超大的市場中缺席。如今總算開發出適用的產品，不過因為是新面孔，先做行銷密集曝光確實有必要。

Monica : Right, do you have any marketing plans to promote this new kit? To be frank with you, we don't have any budget for it in the coming year. You'll have to do it on your own.

對啊，你們有什麼行銷計畫可以推嗎？我得坦白告訴你，VT Taiwan 明年沒預算，你們得自己來喔。

Dr. Lee 解析

> VT Taiwan 並沒有在明年行銷預算中列入 Allen 所要的經費，
> 因此告訴他必須自己想辦法。

Allen : That's bad news. Without promotion, it will definitely <u>take a longer time</u> for us to <u>perform</u>. I'd better work something out with our management for some <u>marketing expenditure</u>.

那真不妙。不先做行銷，會很難賣，得拖上好久才看得出績效。
我得和我的大頭們要行銷經費才行。

Dr. Lee 解析

> Allen 明白行銷非做不可，他得向高層要求預算支援。

Monica : <u>Very much appreciate</u> your efforts. I believe your team will <u>start contributing</u> very soon. I'd like to know more about your marketing plan for this new kit. Our salespeople in Taiwan <u>bumped into</u> some serious <u>headaches</u> <u>while trying</u> to sell this new kit to the dealers. This was the first time they sold instruments along with transducers as a small system.

感恩啦，我相信你的團隊很快就會有成績的。我想多了解你們
對這新組合的規劃。臺灣的業務先前開始推 DQ 顯示器給經銷
商時，也是一個頭兩個大，他們還是第一次賣這種組合小系統。

Dr. Lee 解析

> Monica 也只能口頭鼓勵。不過也很想聽聽 Allen 的計畫，看看 Allen 這邊的作法，是否有什麼能提供同樣正在頭疼的臺灣業務團隊作為參考。

Allen: Oh yes, that's what I'm worrying about too. <u>I myself</u> have had more than 15 years of experience selling <u>measuring instruments</u>. Believe me, it's so different from selling <u>sensing components</u> like transducers. Both our salespeople and our customers need <u>tons of training</u> in order to <u>become familiar with</u> the products and how they work with each other.

對，那也是我現在的煩惱。我自己有超過 15 年賣量測儀錶的經驗，那真的和賣傳感器這種感測零件完全不同。不管是我們業務或是客戶，都需要接受很多教育訓練，才有辦法搞懂二者相互運作的原理。

Dr. Lee 解析

> Allen 將自己多年銷售工業量測元件的經驗分享出來。系統中不同元件，不但功能不同，連銷售方法也很不一樣。因此，無論是自家的業務或是客戶使用單位，都需要接受教育訓練。

Monica: I see. Since the food processing industry in your country is very well known for its <u>advanced</u> processing technology, your successful <u>business model</u> will become an important reference for VT's marketing and salespeople as well as FAE guys in the rest of the world.

是這樣啊。澳洲的食品加工科技，是世界公認超先進的。你們團隊的成功模式，將成為 VT 全球行銷、業務、以及 FAE 的重要參考。

Dr. Lee 解析

各國產業結構與科技水準不盡相同。跨國性工業廠商，經常可截長補短，讓各地行銷業務團隊，能相互學習，彼此支援。

Allen : Well, then you should help us with sufficient marketing funds, right? I'm just kidding. I understand your situation. OK, I'm thinking of attending one of the most influential tradeshows for food processing equipment in Melbourne, in May. We'll have an exhibiting area of 6m x 6m for many application simulations on our booth.

既然這樣，你們更應該多弄些經費資助我們做行銷啊！開玩笑的啦！我了解妳的處境。好，告訴你，我們打算參加五月份在墨爾本舉辦的大型食品加工設備展會。有一個 6m×6m 的展位，可展出各種不同的應用模擬操作。

Dr. Lee 解析

在調侃 Monica 一番後，Allen 表示，他們來年將利用參展機會展出新產品，並利用模擬方式，展示機電結合的產品功能與特性。

Monica : Sounds interesting and I'd really like to be with you guys by then. I'll speak with my new boss, Bob Lee, to see if we should <u>send</u> somebody, either sales or FAE to work with your sales team on your booth. I'll talk to you about this <u>as soon as I have my plans ready</u>.

聽起來就很有趣，我真想到時候能夠去展場。我也會和我新老闆 Bob Lee 討論，看看要不要叫業務或 FAE 去現場見習。有什麼結果，我會再找你談談。

Dr. Lee 解析

大型國際性商展，往往是行銷業務團隊最佳學習機會。能夠面對面接觸客戶，也是推展業務的大好時機。

Allen : Good. And I believe it will be an <u>excellent opportunity</u> for your people to visit the show. I know more than half of the <u>exhibitors</u> are from foreign countries. And many of our competitors will be exhibiting too.

好啊。那會是一個絕佳的參訪機會，因為有超過半數的參展單位來自國外，而且還有很多我們的競爭對手會來參展。

Dr. Lee 解析

國際商展的特色，是參展廠商多元化，並且也會吸引同行競爭廠商。

Monica : Now, let's continue with the new Tier 3 business. We have been working on this in recent weeks. <u>What's your current position?</u>

現在我們繼續來看看第三類市場的新業務吧。我們已經一起研究了好幾星期，你目前覺得如何？

Dr. Lee 解析

顯然第三階市場還有其他機會。

Allen : Oh yes, the <u>concrete batching system</u> business, thanks to the ever increasing investment in construction projects by both public and private sectors. Since now we have a lower-cost version of the SS, IP68 S-type, I'm confident in getting <u>the lion's share</u> of this market.

對哦，預拌混擬土配料系統。多虧政府公部門和私人企業，在各項土木建設的投資不斷增加。而我們現在也成功開發出低價位的不鏽鋼 IP68 S 型傳感器，我有信心在這塊成為龍頭老大。

Dr. Lee 解析

Allen 指出是土木建設必需的預拌混擬土配料系統。正逢澳洲公共建設與房屋建築業轉旺，不愁沒生意機會。加上低價位產品研發成功，Allen 有信心收復失土。

Monica : Yes, competition in this segment has been very <u>fierce</u>. Our model 660 was too expensive to be competitive, and we failed to cut down our production cost. <u>Thanks to</u> the efforts by our development team, the new model 670 <u>is looking real good</u>. I'm so glad that model 670 will help you <u>take back the lost business</u>.

沒錯，這塊市場競爭激烈，我們的 660 太貴沒競爭力，成本又降不下來。幸虧我們開發出低成本的新款 670，相當被看好。這款 670 能幫你們重新奪回市場，可真令人開心。

Dr. Lee 解析

在競爭激烈的產業裡，若要求生存或成長，研發出競爭力強的產品絕對是首要任務。

Allen : I really hope so. These two applications are what we're going to be relying upon for <u>voluminous orders</u>. They are both multi-point applications, especially the concrete batching system. You need at least seven S-types plus one <u>transmitter</u> for one basic system. One of our <u>SI customers</u> already gave us a <u>forecast</u> for 200 systems next year.

但願如此，我們得靠這二種多點系統應用拿到大量的訂單，尤其是預拌混擬土配料系統，每套至少需要 7 支傳感器加上 1 台傳送器。我們有一家系統客戶，已經給我們一整年共 200 套的預估訂單了。

Dr. Lee 解析

第三階市場特性，就是生意量大，但競爭激烈。預拌混擬土系統，又是所謂多點大系統。Allen 已收到客戶的預估訂單，似乎信心十足。

Monica：Congratulations! I'm so excited to hear that. OK, let's move on to Tier 2 business. There is only one target market for you guys, the automated checking machines. Since this is where our profits come from, we are expecting increasing orders from this Tier 2 market.

恭喜啦！我超興奮的。那好，我們來看看第二階市場。Allen，明年你們只有一個目標市場，就是自動檢測設備市場。這將會是我們主要獲利來源，期望你們從這裡拿下更多訂單。

Dr. Lee 解析

真是好消息。Monica 接著討論第二階市場，並指出生意機會是自動檢測設備。對於 VT 來說，這將是利潤希望所在。

Allen：Well, it will be a tough job for us, at least for the time being. You know all of our high speed damper transducers are of analog technology. Currently, most customers are requesting digital dampers. Unless we come up with some sort of incentives, customers won't be interested in our offer.

困難重重，至少目前如此。你也知道，我們所有的高速阻尼傳感器都是類比式，而現今客戶多半都要數位式。因此，除非我

們能提供更多誘因,不然客戶不會有興趣的。

Dr. Lee 解析

雖然多數工業產品生命周期較長,掌握新產品技術趨勢還是很重要。

Monica : I see your point. Our digital dampers are still under testing in our lab and won't be ready to <u>launch</u> until the end of Q2 next year. Besides, the engineering guys are still working on the instruments to go with the digital damper's RS-485 output. In order to get enough business <u>in time</u>, you need to <u>find ways</u> quickly.

我了解這情形。我們的數位阻尼傳感器還在實驗室測試階段,得到明年 Q2 底才可能會完成。況且工程部也還在設計 RS-485 輸入信號的搭配儀錶。為了要及時拿到足夠生意,你們得快點想出辦法才行。

Dr. Lee 解析

VT 開發速度太慢,Allen 必需另想辦法,以現有產品組合加速開拓市場。

Allen : OK, what I can <u>figure out</u> right now is to attack Japanese market, I mean those customers who prefer Japanese instruments such as Nagata or Nishimura. The Japanese systems are still using analog transducers. Our dampers are much better in some critical specifications such as response time, accuracy, humidity protection, and product life. The only problem is price.

好，現在我能想到的辦法，就是進攻日本市場。我的意思是針對那些正在使用日本製 Nagata 或 Nishimura 儀錶的客人。日本系統的傳感器還都是使用類比式，我們的阻尼傳感器在某些決定性規格如速度、精度、防潮能力、和產品壽命等都強上很多，我們只擔心價格。

Dr. Lee 解析

Allen 想主動出擊搶生意，並鎖定特定對象，試圖以優於對手的產品創造出附加價值（value added），唯一擔心的是價格。

Monica: I see. Actually, my understanding of auto checking systems is that speed and accuracy are the two key factors that user customers tend to consider while choosing transducers. Of course, application support and after-sale service are also important. Allen, we have everything, don't we?

這我知道。對自動檢測系統，我實際上了解的是，客戶選傳感器時，最在乎速度與精度，當然應用支援和售後服務也很重要。Allen，這些我們不是都很強嗎？

Dr. Lee 解析

工業產品往往打的是全方位戰，除了靠產品優勢，廠商還得提供完整的應用技術，以及各項售後服務才行。

Allen : I agree with you. However, please bear in mind that we are only selling a part of a system kit to our customers, so there must be enough of an incentive for the user to consider changing components from one vendor to another. It involves a lot of non-commercial factors such as user experience with the operations manual and the calibration procedures. Unfortunately, our system is totally different from that used by the Japanese instruments. Therefore, we need to offer an additional incentive, that is, the better value they're going get against the money they spend.

你說的我同意。但是請別忘了,我們只是賣整套系統的部分零件組給客戶,若要叫他們改用我們的產品,必須要有足夠的誘因才行。要知道,更換零件供應商涉及很多非商業因素,比方說,使用單位對於操作手冊易懂與否,或是校正程序是否繁複的使用經驗。很不幸,在這方面,我們的系統和日本儀錶太不一樣了。所以我們得提供更多誘因,讓這些客戶覺得我們系統的性價比絕對更划算。

Dr. Lee 解析

工業產品另一特色是使用習慣與經驗。這些非商業障礙,往往讓業務感到萬分頭痛。廠商必需付出更多代價,讓客戶感到改變有價值。

Monica : So you think pricing is still very critical in securing the Tier 2 business? I really don't want to see our profits drop in this segment.

你是說,要拿下這塊第二階市場,價格還是很重要囉?但我實

在很不願看到我們在這區塊的利潤減少。

Dr. Lee 解析

第二階市場的業務本來就是要求高利潤，Monica 擔心降價會損害利潤。

Allen : Relax a little bit. I'm fairly optimistic even though there are still some obstacles to overcome. I'm going to send my proposal to you in a couple of days.

別緊張，即便眼前是有些障礙，我還是挺樂觀的。過兩天我會傳建議報告給你。

Dr. Lee 解析

Allen 胸有成竹，已有萬全準備。

Monica : Thanks. I feel better now. Now the Tier 1 business. So far we have been trying hard to identify better opportunities but without a firm conclusion. I need your further input now. Remember, this is where we act like a king. We set the standards for the industry.

謝啦，我覺得輕鬆多了。好，來談談第一階市場，你我至今還沒能找出一個好機會，我想再聽聽你的意見。要記住，在這區塊裡，我們得是制定遊戲規則的老大。

Dr. Lee 解析

至於第一階市場，二人似乎還無共識。畢竟這往往是一個贏家
全拿的區塊。

Allen : I knew you would ask. I suggest that we <u>go after</u> the explosion <u>proof</u> segment. We have a complete line, it is <u>terribly expensive though</u>, yet we are very strong in providing application support for this segment.

我就知道你會問。我建議瞄準防爆這個區塊，畢竟我們已經有
完整產品線，現場應用支援也很強。不過高到不行的售價會是
個大障礙。

Dr. Lee 解析

Allen 還是有計畫，打算用公司最強的一項技術進攻這塊市場。
不過當然有障礙：價格。

Monica : Then why didn't we succeed in the past? ADB has been the leader in the explosion proof market for years. Please don't tell me we lost only because we're too expensive.

那為什麼我們一直賣不好，讓 ADB 當那麼多年老大？可別告
訴我，只是因為我們價格太高的緣故。

Dr. Lee 解析

> Monica 提出質疑，顯然她不太清楚這市場的最新動態。

Allen : Well, unfortunately, yes. Price was the <u>key</u>. I can easily understand why customers are not willing to spend double the money for our top class system when they are satisfied with the ADB system, which is also top class. However, things changed this year when ADB <u>screwed up</u> on a few projects and caused <u>tremendous</u> damage to those customers. They all turned to us for possible co-operation in the coming year.

呃，很不幸，就是這樣沒錯！問題就出在價格。我很能夠理解客戶為什麼不想捨棄現在用得很順手的頂級系統，而要花二倍的錢改用我們頂級系統的理由。不過，今年出現了變化，ADB 搞砸了好幾個案子，造成客戶很大的損失。這些客人就轉向來和我們談明年的合作了。

Dr. Lee 解析

> Allen 解釋過去不成功的原因。然而商機稍縱即逝，唯一的競爭對手出了幾次狀況。VT 必須及時把握住機會取代，成為贏家。

Monica : Really? We need to <u>capitalize on</u> this great opportunity. Send me your detailed proposal next week, OK?

是喔？那我們得好好把握這機會了。下星期把詳細提案傳給我，好嗎？

Dr. Lee 解析

Monica 當然興奮極了。

Allen : I will. Thanks for calling, talk to you.
那一定。謝謝你如此耐心,我們再聊。

Dr. Lee 解析

talk to you 是美語口語說法,等同 "talk to you again soon"。

NOTE

❶ **essential**:必須的、必要的

❷ **distribute**:分配

❸ **resource**:資源

❹ **excel**:勝出、優於
Our team worked so hard to excel in the design competition.
我們團隊拼命贏得設計大賽的首獎。

❺ **tier**:等級、階級

❻ **scale**:規模、比例
I was impressed by the scale of the capital expenditure the company is committing for next year.
我對於這家公司明年即將投入的資本支出規模印象深刻。

NOTE

⑦ geographic region：地理區域

⑧ character or nature：特性或性質

⑨ by doing so：如此一來

By doing so, we are able to widen the technological superiority gap against our competitors.

如此一來，我們將擴大與競爭對手的技術優勢差距。

⑩ systematically：有系統地

⑪ 80/20 principle：80/20 法則或 Pareto 法則

⑫ execute：執行

⑬ manner：方式、風格

We try hard to service our customers in a timely manner.

我們努力嘗試用一種即時回應的方式服務客戶。

⑭ I'm doing great：我好極了

也可用 I'm doing fine. 或 Very good.。

⑮ a number of：一些、有些

Because of the midnight conference call, a number of our sales colleagues came to work late this morning.

由於半夜的電話會議，今天早上有些業務同事很晚才來上班。

⑯ we'd better：我們最好…

為 we had better 的縮寫。

⑰ **time is running short**：時間越來越少

若想表達已經沒時間，則用 time is running out。

⑱ **divide**：分隔、分開

Basically, we divide the market into two major sections i.e., the standard type and the non-standard type.

基本上我們把市場分為二區塊，也就是標準品和非標準品。

⑲ **huge business scale**：龐大的生意規模

scale 規模。

⑳ **weapon**：武器

這裡指用來競爭的適合產品。

㉑ **until now**：至今、到現在

until now 之前常用否定句，I didn't know until now. 我到現在才知道。

㉒ **the other day**：前幾天、幾天前

I remember Susan talked to me about this the other day.

我記得幾天前 Susan 和我討論過這件事

㉓ **aim at**：瞄準、對準

㉔ **IP68**：防護等級 IP68

IP 為 Ingress Protection 的縮寫，是指對使用環境中外物，如粉塵、濕氣、和水的防護等級。

㉕ **transducers**：傳感器、感測器

㉖ **indicator**：顯示器、指示器

NOTE

㉗**since**：用作連接詞時，是既然、由於的意思

Since you're here, it's better to meet up with our team members later today.

既然你來了，最好稍晚能和我們團隊成員見面。

㉘**kit**：在這是指配套組成的產品：傳感器加上顯示儀錶

㉙**to be frank with you**：坦白對你說

㉚**on your own**：自己、獨自

Ian, you'll have to do it on your own.

Ian，你得自己獨自去做。

㉛**take a longer time**：需要較長的時間，較費時

㉜**perform**：表現，指做出績效

㉝**marketing expenditure**：行銷支出

㉞**very much appreciate**：很感激，多用於口語

Lillian, it would be very much appreciated if you could pick me up from the airport.

Lillian，如果妳能來機場接我的話，我會非常感激。

㉟**start contributing**：開始貢獻，表示開始有業績，讓公司獲利。

也能說 start to contribute。

NOTE

㊱ **bump into**：遇上、遇到

也可用 run into。

Our customer bumped into a networking problem with the IR thermometer yesterday.
我們客戶的紅外線溫度儀昨天遇上網路連線問題。

㊲ **headache**：讓人頭疼的問題

㊳ **while trying**：當作連接詞時，這"**while**"指「當…的時候」，而後面子句動詞常用進行式。

She came in while I was trying to call her.
當我正試著打電話給她時，她就來了。

㊴ **I myself**：我自己

「I」的加強語氣。

You are right that I myself made the final decision.
沒錯，是我自己做的最後決定。

㊵ **measuring instruments**：量測儀器

㊶ **sensing components**：感測元件

㊷ **tons of training**：非常多的訓練

也可說 a lot of training 或 lots of training。

㊸ **become familiar with**：對…變得更熟悉

Sandy became a lot more familiar with the return handling procedures.
Sandy 對退貨處理程序變得熟悉多了。

NOTE

44 advanced：進步的、先進的

45 business model：生意（商業）模式

46 sufficient：充足的

We provide our new employees with sufficient training on operation procedures.

我們提供新進員工充分的作業流程訓練。

47 kidding：開玩笑、說笑（口語中常和 be 動詞連用）

You must be kidding me !

你是在開我玩笑吧！

48 attend：（到場）參加

Bob, you're supposed to attend the meeting this afternoon.

Bob，你得參加今天下午的會議。

49 influential：具有影響力的

The trade show in Tokyo last year proved to be influential.

去年的東京展證實了參展的影響力很大。

50 exhibiting area：展出區域，指展位大小

51 booth：攤位、展位

52 send：指派

Don't worry, Allen. We'll send James over to help you.

Allen 別擔心，我們會派 James 去幫助你們。

NOTE

53 **as soon as I have my plans ready**：一旦我計畫好、一旦我準備好

54 **excellent opportunity**：大好機會

55 **exhibit**：（動）參展
exhibitor 參展廠商。

56 **What's your current position?**：你目前有何想法？你目前的情況如何？

57 **concrete batching system**：預拌混凝土配料系統
這裡配料指：砂、碎石、水泥、水、及化學藥劑。

58 **the lion's share**：絕大部分
The good news is that we're enjoying the lion's share of the high-end market.
好消息是我們在高端市場中市佔率最高。

59 **fierce**：激烈、猛烈

60 **thanks to**：由於、歸因於
Our ASP is much higher in our Tier 1 market, thanks to the superior performance of our products.
由於優質的產品特性，我們在第一階市場的平均售價很高。

61 **be looking real good**：看起來真不錯、情況真不錯

62 **take back the lost business**：拿回、搶回丟掉的生意，收復失地的意思

NOTE

⑥③ **voluminous orders**：大訂單（數量或金額）

⑥④ **transmitter**：傳送器

⑥⑤ **SI customers**：系統整合商客戶

SI 是 System Integrator 的縮寫。

⑥⑥ **forecast**：預估、預測

⑥⑦ **target market**：目標市場

⑥⑧ **automated checking machines**：自動檢測機

⑥⑨ **for the time being**：暫時、目前

We don't have to worry about material shortage for the time being.

我們暫時還不需擔心缺料。

⑦⓪ **dampers**：阻尼器

此處是指內建阻尼裝置的傳感器 (damped transducer) 的簡稱。

⑦① **incentives**：誘因、激勵

To most salespeople, sales commission is one of the most important incentives to perform better.

對多數業務人員來說，銷售佣金是做好業績最重要的誘因之一。

⑦② **launch**：新產品推出、發表、或上市

We will launch a series of new switches next month.

下個月我們將推出一系列新交換器。

⑦ in time：及時

準時則用 on time。

⑦ find ways：找出辦法、找到方法

George, the problem is getting worse. You'd better find ways to solve it as quickly as possible.

George，問題越來越嚴重，你最好儘快找出解決辦法。

⑦ figure out：想出、思考出

Cindy, we need to figure out how we can lower our stock level by 50% immediately.

Cindy，我們得想出能立刻將庫存水準降低一半的辦法。

⑦ response time：反應時間

⑦ accuracy：精確度、精準度

⑦ humidity protection：指對濕度、水氣的防護能力

⑦ product life：產品壽命

⑧ tend to：傾向

Nowadays, most manufacturers tend to cut down the number of vendors in order to strengthen their bargaining power.

現今多數製造廠商傾向減少供應商家數，以便增強他們的議價能力。

⑧ of course：當然、自然

⑧ system kit：整機系統的零件組合

NOTE

83 consider changing：考慮改變

提醒：consider 後緊接的動詞，得用動名詞形式。

Please consider changing the price.

請考慮改變價格。

84 non-commercial factors：非商業因素或考量

85 additional：額外的、更多的

86 critical：關鍵性的、決定性的

To become more competitive, capacity is very critical.

若要更具競爭力，產能會是重要關鍵。

87 obstacle：障礙、阻礙

88 overcome：克服、戰勝

89 identify：辨識、辨認

這裡是指「找出」。

It's difficult to identify the root cause of the incident.

很難找出事件發生的根本原因。

90 further input：進一步提供意見

91 set the standards：制定標準

92 go after：追逐、追求

這裡指「進攻」。

93 explosion proof：防爆

NOTE

94 terribly expensive though：儘管貴得要命

though 放在句尾，在口語中較常用。

95 key：關鍵

96 screw up：搞砸、壞事

I'm sorry that I screwed it up.

很抱歉我搞砸了。

97 tremendous：很大的

Michael has been under tremendous pressure.

Michael 的壓力一直很大。

98 capitalize on：利用、把握

Jimmy, we must capitalize on First Metal's insufficient capacity in the next couple of months.

Jimmy，我們一定得把握住未來二個月裡 First Metal 產能不足的機會。

Lesson 4 產品 / 技術藍圖
Product / Technology Roadmap

 課文重點① **Summary 1**

One of the most important tasks for a B2B marketer is to work out a strategic product roadmap continuously for the business. It takes a joint effort from the relevant business functions including sales, marketing, product management and project management, R&D, production engineering, supply chain, and several supporting departments. The product/technology roadmap not only depicts the development path for the target markets but it also serves as an important source of business opportunities for major business partners as well as channel partners.

B2B 行銷部門的核心任務之一,是替公司持續制定策略性產品或技術開發藍圖。產品開發藍圖是企業內各單位,包括業務、行銷、專案管理、研發、生技、供應鏈、以及其他支援單位協同合作、集體努力的結果。產品開發藍圖不但描繪出目標市場的重要開發路徑,往往更是 A 咖客戶或通路夥伴賴以做為開發新生意的重要依據。

產品藍圖：roadmap sharing for solid relationship 4-1

> **Ted**：**Project Manager, Alpha Comm. (Singapore)**：專
> 案經理，新加坡
>
> **Bunny**：**Marketing Manager, Rock Frequency (Taiwan)**：
> 行銷經理，臺灣
>
> **Bunny is visiting Alpha Comm.** Bunny 拜訪 Alpha
> Comm.

Ted： Hi Bunny, <u>since</u> you're here, <u>apart from</u> the sample testing issue, we'd like to know more about your product <u>roadmap</u> for next year.

嗨 Bunny，既然你來了，除了要談的樣品測試，我們還想多了解你們明年的產品開發藍圖。

Bunny： OK, I'll do it now as you guys might be interested in some of our new projects.

好啊，我現在就能說明給你們聽，或許你們會對某些新產品感興趣的。

Ted： You must realize that your roadmap is <u>extremely</u> important to us. Please make sure you always <u>keep us in the loop</u>.

你得了解，貴公司的產品開發藍圖，對我們非常重要，請務必隨時讓我們獲得最新消息。

Bunny： <u>I surely will</u>. Now let me start with the YW7016 that was designed to <u>meet the requirements</u> of your project Hawk.

我一定會的。現在我就從 YW7016 開始吧，那是為你們的 Hawk 專案設計的。

Ted : This is an ongoing project and it looks quite OK so far. We have been working on an extended product using YW7016 with slightly different specs.

這專案正在進行，到目前為止，看起來還不錯。而我們還利用 YW7016，在開發另一規格稍稍不同的延伸產品。

Bunny : Sounds interesting. Please send me the detailed specs to follow up. Meanwhile, you will also see these different items on which we are working as new projects. Most of them are for mobile communication applications.

聽起來挺有趣的，麻煩將詳細規格傳給我，好讓我能追蹤。同時你們還能看到我們新專案的不同品項，絕大多數都是用在行動通訊上的。

Ted : Very impressive, Bunny. We will surely take a serious review of them and get back to you next week. As a matter of fact, we are very interested in that ZK1612 32MHz crystal oscillator as we're also developing a new mobile device.

真讓我們大開眼界，Bunny。我們一定好好研究這些項目，下星期再找你談。實際上，我們對那顆 ZK1612 32MHz 的石英晶體振盪器非常有興趣，因為目前我們也在開發一款新行動裝置。

Bunny : Awesome, I have no problem spending another two hours with you guys. How about taking a 20-minute coffee break now?

太棒了，要我再多花二小時和你們討論都沒問題。我們現在可以先休息 20 分鐘喝杯咖啡嗎？

NOTE

❶ **task**：工作、任務

❷ **strategic**：策略的

❸ **joint efforts**：聯合的力量、共同的努力

It takes joint efforts instead of individual selling skills to win an order of an industrial product.

工業產品的訂單來自集體的努力，而非個人的銷售技巧。

❹ **relevant**：相對應的、相關聯的

❺ **depict**：描繪、描述

The infographics depict the operating procedures of marketing automation.

這些資訊圖描繪出行銷自動化的作業程序。

❻ **path**：途徑、路徑

❼ **serve as**：做為、起…作用

B2B salespeople serve as the interface between two business entities.

B2B 業務人員的作用是扮演兩個企業之間的介面。

❽ **business partners**：生意夥伴，如上游供應商

❾ **channel partners**：通路夥伴，如代理商或經銷商

❿ **since**：既然

Since it's raining hard, why don't we stay here for one night?

既然雨下得那麼大，我們何不在此待上一晚？

⑪ apart from：除開、除了之外

⑫ roadmap：藍圖、路徑圖

⑬ extremely：極端地、非常地

⑭ keep us in the loop：將我們放在訊息圈裡
隨時讓我們了解新發展的意思。

Since the meeting conclusions are very important to our team, please keep us in the loop.

由於會議結論對我們團隊非常重要，一有消息請隨時通知我們。

也能說 keep me posted 或 keep me informed。

Since I'll be on an overseas business trip, please keep me posted of the revised delivery date.

由於我即將出差國外，請務必隨時告訴我修正後的交期。

⑮ I surely will：我一定會的

⑯ meet the requirements：滿足需求、符合需求

⑰ ongoing project：正在進行的專案

⑱ slightly：些微的、少許的

Ray, you're slightly behind your target.

Ray，你還稍稍落後你的目標。

NOTE

⑲follow up：後續追蹤

也可說 sync up。

Eddie, would you please follow up with Chris about the launch date?

Eddie，關於產品上市日期，麻煩你去找 Chris 確認一下。

⑳mobile communication：行動通訊

㉑impressive：令人印象深刻的

㉒take a serious review：認真仔細檢視、檢討

㉓as a matter of fact：事實上

也可說 in fact 或 actually。

As a matter of fact, he was late last night.

事實上，他昨晚遲到了。

㉔device：裝置

㉕how about：「如何」的意思

Andy, how about having a beer tonight?

Andy，晚上一起喝杯啤酒如何？

㉖coffee break：（喝）咖啡休息、短暫休息

課文重點② **Summary 2**

The biggest contribution a B2B marketing team can add to an organization is a strategic product / technology roadmap. A product roadmap may target certain OEM customers who design your product into theirs. It would also address the needs of everyone in the supply chain, from upstream suppliers to downstream channel partners and all the way to end customers. From time to time, there could be point products creating short term wins, especially if they happen to be unique. However, without a strategic product roadmap, customers find themselves lost. All they see is your competitors, because you don't have products occupying those spots.

做好策略性產品藍圖規劃，是 B2B 行銷團隊帶給公司最大的加值與貢獻。雖然有些產品只供應給 OEM 廠商，作為零組件原材料，然而產品藍圖往往也能成為供應鏈每一環節，由上游供應商至下游通路夥伴，一路到終端客戶產品開發的重要依循指標。有時我們的確看到一些較為獨特的單一產品大賣而成為短期贏家。然而如果缺乏一個策略性產品藍圖，將無法與主要往來生意夥伴建立起同步成長機制。倘若公司長期

在這些戰場中缺席，就怪不得客戶放眼望去只看到競
爭對手了。

技術藍圖：roadmap for new development 4-2

Bob : **Marketing VP, Lynden Technology (Taiwan)**：行銷副總，臺灣

Lizzie : **R&D VP, Micro Comm. (U.S.A.)**：研發副總，美國

Tony : **PM VP, Micro Comm. (U.S.A.)**：專案管理副總，美國

Bob's giving a presentation on the product roadmap while visiting Micro Comm., one of his Class 'A' accounts. Bob 拜訪 A 級客戶 **Micro Comm.**，並在會議中簡報公司產品開發藍圖。

 Bob : Good morning, Lizzie, Tony! So nice to see you again and thank you for arranging the meeting today. I'll be showing both of you our product roadmap through the next two years, focusing on the two main items. One is the TCXO for your mobile devices and your red-hot femtocell base station. The other is the OCXO for wireless communications base stations. It may also be a good business opportunity for you to develop.

Lizzie、Tony 早安。能再見面真開心，也謝謝你們安排這次會議。我將會介紹本公司未來兩年的產品開發藍圖，重點會放在二項主力產品。其一是供貴公司行動裝置和正夯的微型基地臺專用的 TCXO。另外就是供無線通訊基地臺使用的 OCXO，這將會是你們拓展生意的好機會。

Dr. Lee 解析

產品藍圖簡報多半直接了當，Bob 先重點說明簡報內容，包含二大項產品開發。

Lizzie: Good. Tony and I have been expecting it for quite a while. I believe we will have a lot to discuss as we've added a few new projects based on what we found from the market.

很好！Tony 和我已經期待好久了。我們根據一些市場資訊，又新增了幾個專案，我相信會有很多可以討論的。

Dr. Lee 解析

客戶研發與 PM 主管對於供應商來訪，介紹關鍵零組件開發藍圖一定很歡迎。

Tony: Right. NexTech has been very aggressive recently, but we prefer to work with you. Glad you're here. Now let's see what you're bringing to us.

沒錯，最近 NexTech 很積極要來談，不過我們比較喜歡和你們配合，真高興你能來。來看看你要帶什麼東西給我們吧！

Dr. Lee 解析

客戶都想引進第二家供應商，以免受限於單一貨源，不易取得有利條件。

Bob ： Thanks very much, and I'm sure we'll <u>beat</u> NexTech in all <u>aspects</u>. I'll begin with our TCXO for smartphones. You can see from the slide, the <u>package size</u> of our TCXO started with the biggest 7.0 x 5.0 x 2.0 mm all the way to the smallest 2.0 x 1.6 x 0.75 mm, with no more than a few years between each step.

謝謝啦。我有自信無論在哪方面，我們都能贏過 NexTech。我就從智慧手機用的 TCXO 說起。這張投影片你們可以看到，我們的 TCXO 由開始最大的封裝尺寸 7.0×5.0×2.0mm，一直到現在最小的 2.0×1.6×0.75mm。每階段相距都只有短短幾年。

Dr. Lee 解析

對於能有機會打入客戶供應鏈，廠商當然也開心。Bob 隨即針對客戶的重點品項開始做介紹，藉由時間序列來顯現公司產品技術提升趨勢。

 Lizzie ： Very <u>impressive</u>. I'm surprised by the speed of <u>miniaturization</u> of the TCXO packages you just showed us. <u>In particular</u>, with the <u>booming</u> global smartphone sales, you <u>scaled</u> the package size <u>down</u> by almost 50% in just four years. That is not easy. <u>So far as I know</u>, NexTech is about 6 months earlier than you.

真厲害！你們 TCXO 的微型化速度之快讓我感到很意外，特別是智慧型手機開始全球大賣，你們有辦法在短短 4 年間將封裝尺寸幾乎減半，真是不簡單。據我所知，NexTech 比你們早了大概半年。

Dr. Lee 解析

技術內容受到對方研發主管肯定，這對供應廠商來說絕對是加分好兆頭。

Tony : I agree with Lizzie. You did a remarkable job with the miniaturization. However, there's a problem we have to deal with immediately, namely the request from Appleton for an even smaller TCXO, to be specific, 1.6 x 1.2 x 0.7 mm, for their new mobile devices. I know one of the Japanese manufacturers has just launched recently. For your information, Appleton's new mobile devices, including a smartphone and a tablet, are scheduled to launch in less than 6 months.

我同意 Lizzie 所說的，你們的微型化做得真棒。不過我們得解決眼前的一個問題，那就是 Appleton 要求我們在他們新行動裝置上用更小的 TCXO，實際尺寸要到 1.6×1.2×0.7 mm，我知道有家日本廠商最近剛推出這款，透露給你參考。Appleton 的新行動裝置，包括一款智慧機和一款平板，預計在半年內就要上市。

Dr. Lee 解析

而 PM 則是在讚許的同時指出眼前待解決的問題，就是得設法滿足現有終端客戶的全新產品需求。雖然 PM 也得考慮零組件成本，但 Tony 的壓力主要來自於上市時間異常緊迫。

Bob : That's what I'm going to elaborate now, i.e., our roadmap for the next two years. You can see from this new slide that <u>in relation to</u> TCXO, we were <u>in the process of</u> evaluating all the <u>options on hand</u>. Basically it's <u>a matter of</u> make or buy.

我正要對你們說明未來二年的產品藍圖。從這張投影片可看出，就 TCXO 來說，這一陣子我們都在評估手中所有選項。基本上，就是到底要自己開發或買技術。

Dr. Lee 解析

Bob 明白 PM 與研發各有不同需求重點，馬上針對 PM 的焦慮對話做出回應。代表這次來訪已做足功課，能立即針對客戶眼前與未來的產品需求提出自家的產品開發藍圖，生意企圖心夠強。工業行銷與業務其實密不可分，抓訂單絕對是最重要的共同目標之一。

Lizzie : <u>Make or buy?</u> I thought you would <u>make your own</u> as usual. After all, it is a tough R&D job. I really <u>wonder where you can buy such a TCXO from</u>. Not from NexTech, <u>for sure</u>.

自己做或向別人買？我想依照往例你們還是會自己開發吧。畢竟那款 TCXO 的研發難度很高，我很懷疑你們還能跟誰買，肯定不會是 NexTech。

Dr. Lee 解析

客戶研發主管對於 Bob 表示有可能以購買技術代替自行開發表示訝異，也質疑可行性。工程人員從技術角度看事情也是正常。

Bob : You're right, not from NexTech. We just acquired a San Francisco-based tech company FoxLab that developed a top-notch TCXO for aerospace-grade telecommunication instruments and an OCXO for telecommunication base stations. They are more than capable of developing TCXOs for industrial applications.

沒錯，當然不是 NexTech。我們剛剛買下一家位於舊金山的科技公司 FoxLab，是一家開發航太等級通訊儀器用 TCXO，以及通訊基地臺用 OCXO 的專業設計製造廠，絕對有足夠能力開發工業應用等級的 TCXO。

Dr. Lee 解析

科技公司之間併購越來越頻繁，擁有獨特技術的小廠常常因緣際會賣到好價錢，也正是大廠快速獲取技術的好方法。

Tony : Great! Then we will have a chance to accept you as the second source. Of course we will have to go through the standard procedure and it takes time. So when will you be able to supply samples, if we provide you with required specs now?

太好了！如此一來，你們就有機會變成第二供應商。當然我們還是得花時間走完標準作業程序才行，如果現在就提供你們所需的技術規格，那要等多久你們才能提供樣品？

Dr. Lee 解析

一看到有機會合作，PM 興奮莫名急著確認何時能開發完成。

Bob : We've just completed the <u>acquisition</u>, however FoxLab <u>has been given the green light</u> to start developing a new TCXO for the <u>next generation</u> mobile devices. In fact, we have held <u>intensive</u> meetings recently for different purposes. In terms of <u>development lead time</u>, we are <u>aiming at</u> 5 to 8 weeks for the <u>reference design</u>.

我們才剛完成收購程序，不過 FoxLab 已經得到授權進行開發新一代行動裝置用的 TCXO。事實上，最近我們密集開了各種會議，就參考設計所需開發時間來說，我們的目標是 5 到 8 週。

Dr. Lee 解析

雖然已完成併購，能夠順利運作還是最重要的。參考設計對於研發專業公司來說通常都不是大問題。

 Lizzie : I know Tony is more concerned about the timing of the testing samples, but from the R&D point of view, I only care about the oscillator's <u>overall performance</u>, nothing else. Yes, NexTech <u>charged</u> unreasonably high prices for their MM1612 TCXO, but I'm really satisfied with its performance. It made our developing work <u>a lot easier</u>. <u>Trouble shooting</u> and <u>debugging</u> always <u>drives us nuts</u>.

我知道 Tony 更擔心何時能測試樣品。不過從研發角度來說，我只在意震盪器的整體表現而已。沒錯，NexTech 的 MM1612 TCXO 貴得離譜，但是我非常滿意它的特性表現。它使我們開發工作變得簡單多了，要知道偵錯除錯會把我們研發工程師搞瘋掉。

Dr. Lee 解析

客戶研發的 Lizzie 還是強調研發最在意的，還是新零組件能否
對研發工作有幫助，取得成本只是次要考慮因素。因此對於現
有獨家供應商的高單價還能接受。

☺ **Bob**: I see your point, Lizzie, and I can't agree more. I talked
with FoxLab's R&D head yesterday and we came up with a
conclusion that he himself and two senior engineers will be
visiting you, most likely in two weeks. They intend to meet
your team members and discuss with you face to face. I'm
confident that you'll be pleased with what they can offer you
regarding TCXO.

Lizzie，我懂你的意思，也非常贊同你的想法。我昨天和 Fox-
Lab 的研發長談過，並決定由他本人和二位資深工程師前來拜
訪，時間很可能會在二星期內。他們打算和你們團隊成員進行
面對面討論，相信你們絕對會滿意他們在 TCXO 方面帶來的
協助。

Dr. Lee 解析

Bob 顯然信心滿滿，並且已安排好後續動作，讓研發主管率隊
前來拜訪與客戶端研發團隊面對面討論。這顯示身為行銷主
管，必須得跳脫單一行銷角度而能全方位考量才行。Bob 能充
分掌握客戶動態，也是由於日常與業務單位密切互動的結果。

☺ **Tony**: Lizzie is right that I'm worrying about time-to-market the most. After all, I am the one who will be held responsible for the success of this project. Actually, we have two projects, smartphone and tablet, using the 1612 type of TCXO. I'm very excited to know that your TCXO engineers are coming to work with us. I'll surely take part in the discussion and hope we'll be able to get good results in the end. Nevertheless, being the responsible PM, I find it difficult to accept 5 to 8 weeks lead time.

Lizzie 說的完全正確，我最擔心的是產品能否準時上市，畢竟到頭來負責案子成敗的是我。實際上我們有智慧手機和平板二項專案會用到 1612 的 TCXO，真的很高興你們的 TCXO 工程師要來和我們一起工作，我一定會參加討論的，更希望最後會有好結果。不過話說回來，身為專案負責人，我很難接受 5 到 8 週的開發期。

Dr. Lee 解析

身為 PM 的 Tony 再次強調嚴格控管專案進度責任的重要性，對於廠商所提出的開發時間無法接受。

Bob : All right, Tony, I get your point. Don't worry too much about the lead time now. Things may change after they get here as they will know your demand a lot better by then.

好的，Tony，我了解你的意思。現在不用太擔心開發時間長短，等他們來訪後，或許因為更了解你們的需求，情形就可能不一樣了。

Dr. Lee 解析

供應商 Bob 表示理解，並且相信問題能順利解決。

Lizzie : Yes, I agree with you, Bob. I guess just like our R&D engi-neers, they may <u>tend to be conservative</u> when they don't see the <u>whole picture</u>. Anyway, we are <u>eager</u> to meet them.

是的 Bob，我同意你的說法。我認為他們就像我們研發工程師一樣，在沒能全盤了解狀況前會傾向持保守態度。無論如何，我們很渴望和他們見面。

Dr. Lee 解析

研發的 Lizzie 則期盼雙方研發團隊能早日碰頭。

Tony : Lizzie, please make sure that you keep me in the loop, OK? Now, how about femtocell? The latest market development of femtocell focuses on the decreasing price level <u>as a conse-quence of</u> <u>loosening regulation</u>. Therefore I need to <u>bring one thing up</u>, i.e., the customers are asking a much lower price of TCXO, from the previous $8 to <$2 now. So far NexTech <u>hasn't taken any action yet</u>, however a few of their existing customers came to us with RFQs. What's your plan, Bob?

Lizzie，請務必隨時讓我知道進展啊！現在可以談 Femtocell 了嗎？由於相關法規的放寬，市場最新的發展聚焦在 Femto-cell 單價的下滑。因此我得提出一點，就是客戶端也在要求更便宜的 TCXO，從原來的 $8 降到現在 <$2。目前 NexTech 還

按兵不動，不過他們幾家現有客戶找上我們要求報價。Bob，你們有何規劃呢？

Dr. Lee 解析

此時 PM Tony 提出另一頭痛的產品售價問題，這是由於法規鬆綁而導致終端產品規格變動所造成。PM 受到最終端客戶的壓力，必須降低零組件取得成本而向廠商 Bob 提出降價要求。

Bob : We learned only last month about the changes in femtocell specifications. Technically we don't have any problem. Product-wise, I believe there will be two categories of femtocell, namely the original high end version and the modified low end version. With regard to the pricing, we haven't yet completed the calculation since our R&D team hasn't finished the testing of the low end TCXO. I believe NexTech is facing the same situation.

我們一直到上個月才知道 Femtocell 改了規格。我們在技術上完全沒問題，而在行銷上我認為未來會有二種不同等級的 Femtocell：一是原有規格的高階版本，一是放寬規格的低階版本。至於定價，由於研發團隊還沒完成低階版的 TCXO 測試，我們也還無法制定價格。我相信 NexTech 也面臨相同情況。

Dr. Lee 解析

廠商表示更改規格不成問題，但對於降價則選擇觀望拖延暫不評論。

Lizzie : I would say it's not a good sign, because now everybody would think that a femtocell should be a cheap base station device. Then all the manufacturers will be forced to compete by pricing, just like many other networking devices such as switches and routers. We engineers love to design high-end products with higher margins. After all, engineers are quite expensive.

這不是個好現象。因為現在大家都會認為 Femtocell 應該是廉價的基地臺，就如同其他網通產品如交換器和路由器那樣，導致每家製造廠商被迫得低價競爭。其實我們工程師喜歡設計高階高利潤產品，畢竟工程師挺貴的。

Dr. Lee 解析

研發工程師的直爽但嚴謹的態度表露無疑，Lizzie 對於這種降低工程嚴謹度的結果感到憂心。

Tony : I totally concur with Lizzie. The femtocell project in our company has been highly expected by our management as an important profit source this year. You know something? I'm counting on it for my next raise, and also my whole career development. It may sound like I am exaggerating, but for sure I'm <u>under tremendous pressure</u>. We've been constantly reviewing the BOM <u>in the hope that</u> we get more business on one hand and higher profitability on the other.

我完全同意 Lizzie 說的。一直以來公司高層對於 Femtocell 專案期望很高,認為是今年一個重要獲利來源。但你們知道嗎?我今年加薪甚至未來職涯發展全靠它了。聽起來有些誇張,但我的壓力確實大到不行。我們隨時都在檢討料表,一方面希望能增加營收,另一方面也希望能提高獲利率。

Dr. Lee 解析

最終專案賺不賺錢,PM 責任最大,Tony 表示自己前途就由這些專案對公司的貢獻度高低來決定,也因此對於成本與時間特別敏感。

Bob

: OK, we've had a great roadmap discussion on TCXO already. Before we <u>leave for</u> lunch, I'd like to spend a few minutes on our OCXO if you don't mind. I know currently you don't have any base station equipment business. But you'll find this could be <u>the most promising</u> business opportunity to <u>pursue</u> in the near future. The OCXO <u>know-how</u> is a lot more complicated and difficult than any other types of oscillators, including TCXO.

不錯,剛剛我們這段 TCXO 藍圖討論真讚。如果二位不介意,在我們出去用中餐前我想花幾分鐘介紹 OCXO。我了解現階段你們並沒有基地臺設備的生意,但你們會發現,這個市場會是你們短期未來可考慮追求的最佳商機。OCXO 技術遠比其他任

何種類的震盪器包括 TCXO 複雜，也困難得多。

Dr. Lee 解析

至此，Bob 已完成重點產品藍圖介紹，但還想利用機會對客戶裡的關鍵人物（研發與 PM）簡短介紹因公司併購而產生的新商機：通訊基地臺的高階石英震盪器 OCXO。

Tony : Wait, wait, Bob. Are you saying you're able to supply OCXO now? We've been approached by XTE recently for possible ODM base station projects. The nominated OCXOs were from Luketron.

等等 Bob，你是說現在你們也賣 OCXO？最近 XTE 公司也在找我們談可能的基地臺 ODM 案子，震盪器部分指定要用 Luketron 的 OCXO。

Dr. Lee 解析

PM 握有公司各項專案相關的資訊，包括許多尚未成案的生意訊息。對於廠商的新產品動態當然必須密切注意，立刻對 Bob 所提的 OCXO 產生極大興趣。

Bob : That's great! And yes, we are able to supply OCXO now, direct from FoxLab. As a matter of fact, FoxLab has been famous for supplying NASA with a customized OCXO over a long period of time. Definitely they are able to make industrial grade OCXOs for the base station application. I'll be sending some more information to you two <u>upon my return</u> next Monday.

太棒了！沒錯，現在我們也能直接從 FoxLab 供應 OCXO。實際上，FaxLab 多年來是以供應 NASA 客製 OCXO 出名，絕對有能力供應工業等級基地臺的 OCXO。我下週一回臺後就馬上寄一些資料給你們。

Dr. Lee 解析

無心插柳柳成蔭，讓 Bob 有些意外。這種現象在人員親自到場拜訪時經常會遇上，Bob 當然樂意回去立即處理。

Lizzie : Bob, you came through <u>with perfect timing</u>. We definitely want to work with you for the base station projects as Tony just said. Please make sure to ask your <u>colleagues</u> in FoxLab to contact me before visiting us. We'd better <u>proceed to dialogue</u> ASAP.

Bob，你來的正是時候。就像 Tony 說的，我們當然願意在基地臺案子上和你們合作，也請你務必讓 FoxLab 稍後要來的同事馬上和我聯繫，我們得儘早開始對話。

Dr. Lee 解析

研發的 Lizzie 則對 Bob 適時來說明產品藍圖感到滿意，並且希望合作腳步加快。

☺ **Bob**：I will surely do. I'm so excited now. OK, let's go and eat!
一定辦到，我太興奮了！好，吃飯去！

Dr. Lee 解析

Bob 顯然很滿意會議結果且興奮不已。

NOTE

❶add to：加至、加上、補充

Application support is what we can add to our core product to create highest customer value.
應用支援是我們能加在核心產品上，創造出最高客戶價值的服務。

❷product / technology roadmap：產品 / 技術開發藍圖

❸address：處理
也可用 deal with。

❹supply chain：供應鏈

❺upstream：上游的

Sharp Precision is one of our important upstream business partners.
Sharp Precision 是我們重要的上游生意夥伴之一。

6 downstream：下游的
是 upstream 的反義字。

7 from time to time：有時、偶爾
Bob, from time to time we ran into trouble too.
Bob，有時我們也會碰上麻煩。

8 point product：單一產品，指單獨為某一功能而設計
的產品

9 happen to：碰巧、偶然
Lily, I happened to find this resistor on the LinkedIn page.
Lily，我偶然在 LinkedIn 頁面上看到這顆電阻。

10 unique：獨特的

11 lost：迷失的、走失的、不知所措的

12 occupy：占據、占有
Felix, currently Tecktron is occupying the entire top tier of the
market pyramid.
Felix，現階段 Tecktron 獨占市場金字塔頂端區塊。

13 spot：位置、地點

14 Class 'A' accounts：A 級客戶
也是 80/20 原理所指 20% 的重點客戶。

15 focus on：聚焦、專注

NOTE

⑯**TCXO**：溫度補償石英震盪器

為較高階石英震盪器一種，現多用於智慧型手機或微型基地臺。

⑰**mobile devices**：行動上網裝置、如智慧型手機與平板電腦

⑱**red-hot**：火熱的

指當今極受歡迎的。

Anita, do you think the new iPhone will become red-hot when Apple launches next week?

Anita，下星期 Apple 推出新 iPhone，你認為會大賣嗎？

⑲**femtocell base station**：毫微型通訊基地臺

泛指超小型基地臺。

⑳**OCXO**：恆溫石英震盪器

為現今最高階石英震盪器，多用在無線通訊基地臺設備上。

㉑**wireless communications**：無線通信或通訊

㉒**develop**：開發

㉓**quite a while**：相當一段時間、有一陣子了

I've been watching him for quite a while.

我一直觀察他好一陣子了。

NOTE

㉔ **based on**：根據、依據

Bruce deserves a raise based on his sales performance in the past 18 months.

根據過去 18 個月的業績表現，Bruce 應該加薪。

㉕ **aggressive**：積極主動的、有侵略性的

Linda, you have to be more aggressive in getting orders.

Linda，你得更加積極去接單。

㉖ **prefer to**：寧願或更喜歡

I know it's cheaper, but I prefer to buy a better one.

我知道那個比較便宜，不過我寧願買一個較好的。

I prefer jazz to heavy metal.

我喜歡爵士樂更勝重金屬樂。

㉗ **bring to**：帶來

㉘ **beat**：戰勝、擊敗

Nick, I don't think we'll beat ZM's super low price.

Nick，我不認為我們有辦法報出比 ZM 超低價更低的價格。

㉙ **aspect**：方面

Becky, we need to look at all aspects of this problem.

Becky，我們得從多方面來看這問題。

㉚ **package size**：封裝尺寸

NOTE

㉛impressive：令人印象深刻的

Terry, MTK's Michael told me your presentation this morning was very impressive.

Terry，MTK 的 Michael 告訴我說你今早的簡報令他印象非常深刻。

㉜miniaturization：微型化、小型化

㉝in particular：特別地、尤其

She loves to drink wine; red wine, in particular.

她愛喝酒，特別是紅酒。

㉞booming：激增的、快速發展的

㉟scale … down：縮小

Because of the ever decreasing profit margin, we need to scale the marketing expenditures down in the future.

由於毛利日益減少，未來我們必須減少行銷支出。

㊱by almost 50%：(接上句) 幾乎達**50%**

介系詞用 by 表示程度多寡。

㊲so far as I know：據我所知

David didn't get the order, so far as I know.

據我所知，David 並沒拿到訂單。

㊳agree with：同意、贊成

I agree with what John just said.

我同意 John 剛才的說法。

㊳ remarkable：非常好的、了不起的

The design-win was made possible by some remarkable team-work among engineering, marketing, and sales.

透過工程、行銷、和業務了不起的團隊合作，才有辦法拿到這設計承認訂單。

㊵ deal with：處理、解決

It's a serious problem. We need to deal with it right now.

這問題很嚴重，我們得立即處理。

㊶ even smaller：更小的

Even + 形容詞比較級，表示「更⋯」意思。

Susan, your car is even smaller than that of your brother!

Susan，妳的車甚至比妳哥的車還小！

㊷ specific：具體的、特定的

Please be more specific, Abby.

Abby，妳得說得更具體些。

㊸ launch：發動、發射

指新產品上市發表。

㊹ for your information：提供訊息供你參考

For your information, Debbie won't be coming tonight.

這個消息給你參考，Debbie 今晚不會來。

NOTE

45 schedule：安排、排定

Don, the kickoff meeting is scheduled for tomorrow afternoon.

Don，啓動會議安排在明天下午。

46 elaborate：闡述、詳細說明

Neil, would you please elaborate on that?

Neil，你能再詳細說明這點嗎？

47 in relation to：關於

Brenda, in relation to their aggressiveness, what's your action plan now?

Brenda，對於他們的積極搶單，妳現在有什麼行動方案？

48 in the process of：在…過程中

We are still in the process of evaluating your proposal.

我們還在評估你的提案中。

49 evaluate：評估、評核

50 options on hand：手中握有的選項

Vincent, at this point we don't have too many options on hand.

Vincent，目前我們手中沒有太多選項。

51 a matter of：是…的問題

We will win; it is just a matter of time.

我們會贏的，只是遲早的問題

52 make or buy：自製或外購

NOTE

53 make your own：自行生產

Make (our/your/their) own。

We always make our own testing jigs.

我們的測試夾具都自己做。

54 as usual：照例、依照往常

55 wonder：懷疑、好奇、想知道

I wonder how much you paid for the dinner tonight?

我很好奇今天晚餐花了你多少錢。

56 where you can buy such a TCXO from：你們
能從哪裡買到這類**TCXO**

*這裡學二種不同說法：除了可把 from 放在句尾，也可把 from 放在 where
的前面，而成為 from where you can buy such a TCXO？*

Do you mind telling me where you bought this stopwatch from?

你介意告訴我在哪買到這隻碼錶嗎？

I wonder, from where you bought that lovely vase?

我很好奇你是從哪裡買到那支可愛的花瓶？

57 for sure：確定、一定

Jessie, I'll come and visit you next week, for sure.

Jessie，我下星期一定會去拜訪妳。

58 acquire：獲得、收購

NOTE

59 San Francisco-based：位於舊金山的，或登記、註冊在舊金山的

DSMC is Hsinchu-based, and is the world's largest dedicated semiconductor foundry.

DSMC 是一家位於新竹，全球規模最大的一家半導體專業代工廠。

60 tech company：科技公司

technology company 的簡稱。

61 top-notch：頂尖的、一流的

Ray, these guys are top-notch engineers.

Ray，這些傢伙都是頂尖的工程師。

62 aerospace-grade：航太等級的

63 instrument：儀器

64 more than capable：非常有能力

Sandra, I believe your team is more than capable of providing quality customer service.

Sandra，我相信妳的團隊絕對能提供優質客服的。

65 second source：指第二供貨來源、廠家

Vicky, we'd better find a second source for TCXO quickly.

Vicky，我們最好趕緊找另一家 TCXO 供應商。

66 go through：通過、經過

The instrument has to go through a complete testing procedure in order to get it approved.

這儀器得通過一套完整的測試程序才能得到認證。

67 it takes time：需要時間

It takes time for a rookie to become familiar with the internal procedures.

一位新人需要時間去熟悉內部程序。

68 provide someone with：提供…給某人

Barbara provided her boss with what she found on the internet.

Barbara 將網路上找到的資訊提供給她老闆。

69 specs：規格

specifications 的縮寫。

70 acquisition：獲得、收購

acquire 的名詞。

The acquisition proved successful.

那收購案後來證實是成功的。

71 has been given the green light：已經得到許可、已經被允許

Andy has been given the green light to attend the conference.

Andy 已被允許參加會議了。

NOTE

72 next generation：下個世代

73 intensive：密集的

Stop worrying, Ethan. I'll give Mia some intensive training to make sure that she knows more about manufacturing.

Ethan，別再擔心啦！我會給 Mia 密集訓練，好讓她更了解製造。

74 development lead time：開發完成所需時間

75 aim at：以…為目標

We are aiming at achieving a 20% growth in revenue.

我們以達成 20% 營收成長率為目標。

76 reference design：參考設計

常見的公板設計就屬參考設計的一種。

To save development resource, many companies choose to adopt the reference design.

為了節省研發資源，許多企業選擇採用參考設計。

77 overall performance：整體表現

78 charge：收費

此處指定價。

NOTE

⑦⑨ **a lot easier**：更加簡單

也可說 much easier。

It is a lot easier to talk about the roadmap than to execute it.
產品藍圖，說要比做簡單多了。

⑧⓪ **trouble shooting**：偵錯、找出問題點並加以排除

⑧① **debugging**：偵錯、找出問題點並加以排除（多半針
對電腦程式編寫或電子硬體設計）

Samuel, very often it takes double the efforts to do debugging or
trouble shooting.
Samuel，偵錯除錯往往得耗費加倍的精力。

⑧② **drive us nuts**：把我們逼瘋、抓狂

口語常用。也可說 drive us bananas。

The shipping delay drove my customer nuts.
延遲出貨把我的客戶逼瘋了。

⑧③ **I see your point**：我明白你的意思

⑧④ **can't agree more**：再同意不過了、非常同意

⑧⑤ **come up with a conclusion**：提出、做出結論

We came up with a conclusion to stop buying laptops from Akton immediately.
我們做出結論，立即停止向 Akton 採購筆電。

NOTE

86 senior：資深的、職位高的

87 most likely：可能、大概

David, most likely we'll have our high-speed digital damper 330 ready in 4 weeks.

David，我們高速數位阻尼器330大概能在4星期內開發完成。

88 intend to：打算、意圖

We don't intend to compete by undercutting competitors.

我們不打算削價競爭。

89 face to face：面對面、當面

Jack, we need to talk face to face.

Jack，我們得面對面談。

90 be pleased with：對…感到滿意、高興

George, I'm pleased with what you did for the entire team.

George，我很滿意你對整個團隊的付出。

91 time-to-market：上市時機

嚴格是指從產品概念形成，到上市銷售所需的時間。

92 the most：最

What I care the most about is product quality.

我最在意的是產品品質。

93 be held responsible：為…負責任

Larry will be held responsible for failing to achieve the sales target.
Larry 將為沒能達成銷售目標負責。

94 take part in：參加

也可用 participate in。

All the salespeople took part in the regional sales meeting.
所有業務人員都參加了區域業務會議。

95 in the end：終究、最後、到後來

96 I find it difficult：我覺得…困難

*這種句型常用到，困難是指緊跟著「difficult」後面那件事情。就拿這句
「Nevertheless, being the responsible PM, I find it difficult to accept 5 to 8
weeks lead time.」來看，是指「to accept 5 to 8 weeks lead time」(接受 5
到 8 週的開發期) 很困難。*

I find it so inefficient to go back and forth confirming with the
planner about delivery dates.
我覺得來來回回和生管確認交期實在很沒效率。

97 tend to be conservative：傾向保守

Contrary to most engineers, very few salespeople tend to be
conservative.
和工程師相反，有保守傾向的業務人員非常少。

98 whole picture：全貌

也可說 full picture 或 big picture。

NOTE

99 eager to：渴望、盼望

Henry, we're eager to see the robotic arm designed by your team for automatic testing.

Henry，我們好期望能看到你們團隊設計的自動測試用機械手臂。

100 as a consequence of：因而、由於…的結果

As a consequence of the poor product quality, the company has received strong complaints from its customers.

由於產品品質不良，公司已經接獲客戶的強烈抱怨。

101 loosening regulation：漸漸放寬的法規

102 bring one thing up：提出一件事情

Taking this opportunity I'd like to bring one thing up.

藉此機會，我想提出一件事。

103 haven't taken any action yet：尚未採取行動

原形 take action，採取行動。

Facing the price war initiated by Apex, so far the company hasn't taken any action yet.

面對 Apex 公司掀起的價格戰，到目前為止，公司還沒採取任何行動。

NOTE

104 product-wise：產品方面

Product-wise, our focus is on high-end intrinsically safe, ATEX approved instruments.

在產品方面,我們聚焦在高端本質安全,歐盟 ATEX 認證儀器。

105 category：品類、種類

106 with regard to：關於、有關

也可直接用 regarding。

With regard to the pricing, I'll let you know later today.

關於定價,我今天稍晚會告訴你。

107 face the same situation：面臨相同情形

108 it's not a good sign：不是好現象、不是好前兆

Dennis, it's not a good sign to fall behind your target by such a large percentage.

Dennis,如此大幅度落後目標不是好現象。

109 be forced to compete by pricing：被迫打價格戰、不得不以低價競爭

Ryan, for some commodity items, we'll be forced to compete by pricing.

Ryan,對於幾項大宗產品,我們被迫得採取價格戰。

110 networking devices：網通裝置

NOTE

⑪**switch and router**：交換器與路由器

⑫**margin**：泛指毛利或毛利率

Allison, our average margin has been declining.

Allison，我們的平均毛利率一直在下降。

⑬**concur with**：贊同

與 agree with 意思相同。

⑭**count on**：仰賴、依賴

We are counting on Sandra to work out a solution to the problem.

我們仰賴 Sandra 想出解決問題的方法。

⑮**raise**：加薪、調薪

What happened to Owen? Not happy about the raise?

Owen 怎麼啦？不爽加薪嗎？

⑯**career development**：職涯發展

⑰**exaggerate**：誇大、誇張

Brandon might have been exaggerating, but he didn't lie.

Brandon 或許有些誇張，但是他沒說謊。

⑱**under tremendous pressure**：承受極大壓力

⑲**in the hope that**：希望

We decided to increase our ASP in the hope that we will generate more profits by the end of year.

我們決定調高平均售價，希望到年底時能有更多利潤。

NOTE

⑳ **leave for**：去、前往

My boss and I will leave for Singapore tomorrow.

我和我老闆明天要去新加坡。

㉑ **the most promising**：最有希望的、最被看好的

The Tier 2 market contains some of the most promising industries, such as automotive electronics and networking devices.

第二階市場包括好幾類最被看好的產業，如車用電子和網通設備產業。

㉒ **pursue**：追求、從事經營

e-Business has been a promising money-making opportunity for young people to pursue.

電子商務一直是年輕人追求財富的好機會。

㉓ **know-how**：專門技術

㉔ **approach**：接近

這裡指聯繫接觸的意思。

Lucas, did you approach Maria of JDR to follow up on their latest complaint?

Lucas，你有聯繫 JDR 的 Maria 追蹤他們最近的客訴嗎？

㉕ **ODM**：原廠設計代工製造

Original Design Manufacturing 之縮寫。

NOTE

⑫⑥ **nominate**：指定

Mr. Landry nominated Ian as the chief project leader of the Xavier 77.

Landry 先生指定 Ian 擔任 Xavier 77 的首席專案經理。

⑫⑦ **famous for**：以 … 聞名

DSMC has been famous for its advanced manufacturing capability.

DSMC 一直以先進製造能力聞名。

⑫⑧ **over a long period of time**：一段長時間

⑫⑨ **upon my return**：我返回後就立刻…

I'll call you upon my return next Wednesday.

等下週三我一回去就打電話給你。

⑬⓪ **with perfect timing**：在一個完美的時間點上，時機恰好

⑬① **colleague**：同事

⑬② **proceed to dialogue**：進行對話

Dylan, I suggest that you proceed to dialogue with the customer immediately.

Dylan，我建議你立即和客戶談談。

Lesson 5

產品組合與開發
Product Mix & Development

課文重點① **Summary 1**

Setting up a new product roadmap is <u>essentially</u> the <u>core</u> of marketing for many industrial products, <u>either</u> in traditional <u>or</u> in <u>contemporary</u> high-tech industries. Most of the new product developments <u>originate</u> from new market demand. As a result, marketing and sales people need to <u>stay close</u> to their customers and be <u>sensitive</u> to the <u>subtle</u> changes in market demand. <u>In practice</u>, offering an <u>optimal</u> <u>product mix</u> to different channel partners and <u>effectively</u> <u>managing</u> it are becoming more important for marketing and sales people than <u>ever before</u>.

對於許多工業產品，無論屬傳統產業或屬現代高科技產業來說，行銷的工作核心就是制定新產品開發藍圖。多數新產品開發源自市場新需求，行銷業務人員就得更接近客戶，並且能敏銳察覺出市場需求的些微變化。而在日常行銷作業上，針對不同的通路夥伴，提供最適當的產品組合，也變得越來越重要。

產品組合分配：multiple channel management 5-1

Anita：**Marketing & Sales Manager, ATE Inc. (Taiwan)**：
行銷業務經理，臺灣

Daniel：**General Manager, States Precision (ATE's distributor in Thailand)** 總經理，ATE 泰國總代理

Video conference 視訊會議

Anita：Good morning, Daniel. We're here to discuss our <u>new product development plan</u> and the <u>product offering plan</u> of next year.

早安 Daniel，我們在這兒要討論新產品開發計畫，以及明年能提供的產品組合。

Daniel：Good morning, Anita, good to hear that, as we have been <u>carrying</u> and selling the <u>existing lines</u> for too long.

早安 Anita，聽妳這麼說真好。我們經銷現有產品線已經太久了！

Anita：I understand and that's why we are so <u>eager to</u> share our new product details with you before officially <u>launching</u> them in the next quarter.

我了解，那就是我們為何在下一季正式推新產品前，亟需和你分享相關細節的原因。

Daniel：I can see there are <u>quite a few</u> new or modified products in your plan. Please tell us how you're going to <u>assign</u> them between the other two dealers and ourselves.

在這計畫裡,我看到不少新產品和改版品。麻煩妳告訴我,在我們和另二家經銷商之間,你要如何分配這些產品?

Anita : We have a <u>thorough</u> <u>channel plan</u> to <u>accommodate</u> the specific requirements of each dealer, so don't worry too much.

我們已經做好一份完整的通路規劃,將可以滿足每家經銷商各別的需求,所以不必太擔心。

Daniel : We <u>are concerned about</u> the <u>severe competition</u> among all three of your dealers. It happened last time with the TD 1100 series, remember?

我們擔心三家經銷商之間嚴重的競爭,上次的 TD 1100 系列就是這樣啊,妳還記得嗎?

Anita : Of course I remember, however, it won't happen this time. We have <u>run through</u> our computer systems to do the most reasonable assignment. And we found there would not be too much competition if you all <u>follow rules</u>.

我當然記得,不過這次不會了。我們按照電腦管理系統裡的數據與資料,做最合理的分配。如果一切正常,我認為你們經銷商之間應該不會出現激烈的競爭。

Daniel : Oh you just mentioned that <u>magic word</u>, 'if'. I have to further <u>investigate</u> your plan with our sales team before making any comments.

噢,你剛剛說到了關鍵字:「如果」。我得再和我的業務團隊一起研究妳的計畫才能做決定。

Anita : Great, just <u>take your time</u> reviewing it. We'll talk about this next time.

太好了!不急,你們可以慢慢研究,我們下次再談。

NOTE

❶ essentially：實質上

Product development is essentially a major part of the B2B marketing mission.

實際上，B2B 行銷的重要工作是產品開發。

❷ core：核心、中心

❸ either…or…：或…、不是…就是

Alex, either Michael or Nathan is to attend the seminar with you tomorrow.

Alex，Michael 或 Nathan 其中一個明天會和你一起參加研討會。

❹ contemporary：當代的、同時代的

Many contemporary technologies help industrial marketers become more effective.

工業行銷人員藉由許多現代科技而變得更有效率。

❺ originate：源自、起源於

The humidity-proof enclosure of model 330 originated from purge/pressurization technology.

330 機型的防潮外箱設計源自吹淨增壓技術。

❻ stay close：靠近、貼近

The best way for a marketer to stay close to the market is to become a salesperson.

讓行銷人員貼近市場最好的方法就是去當業務。

⑦ **sensitive**：敏感的

⑧ **subtle**：細微的、微妙的、敏感的

⑨ **in practice**：實際上、實務上

In practice, product managers are being held fully responsible for the success of the new products.

實務上，產品經理須對新產品開發成敗負全責。

⑩ **optimal**：最佳的、最適的

As a matter of fact, being optimal is even harder than being maximal.

事實上，追求最佳結果要比追求最大結果更困難。

⑪ **product mix**：產品組合

⑫ **effectively**：有成效地

⑬ **manage**：管理

Hey guys, please make sure that you are managing your time effectively.

各位，請務必確實做好時間管理。

⑭ **ever before**：以往、以前任何時候

Eric, we are much busier than ever before.

Eric，我們現在比以往更忙。

⑮ **new product development plan**：新產品開發計劃

NOTE

⑯ **product offering plan**：產品提供計畫

offering 在此是指廠商如何針對不同經銷商,「提供」不同產品組合,以利經銷商銷售。

⑰ **carry**：並不是攜帶的意思,而是指經銷商手中所「經銷」的產品線

XYZ Computers is carrying a complete line of laptops including HP, Asus, Toshiba, Sony, Lenovo, and many others.

XYZ 電腦門市經銷各品牌筆電,包括 HP、Asus、Toshiba、Sony、Lenovo,及其他品牌 。

⑱ **existing lines**：指現階段經銷的產品線

⑲ **eager to**：渴望、熱切期望

Simon, we are eager to meet you at the marketing seminar tomorrow morning.

Simon,我們渴望在明天上午行銷研討會上見到你。

⑳ **launch**：上市、推出、發表

Pete, we're going to launch the G5 controller in two weeks.

Pete,我們將在二星期內推出 G5 控制器。

㉑ **quite a few**：不少、許多

NOTE

㉒ **assign**：指派、分派

廠商放給多家經銷商銷售，會根據不同考量，將不同產品組合分配給各經銷商。

Nicholas, we'll assign the G4 instruments and PHS IR thermometers to Systec.

Nicholas，我們會把 G4 儀表和 PHS 紅外線溫度儀給 Systec 經銷。

㉓ **thorough**：詳盡的、完整詳細的

㉔ **channel plan**：通路計畫

㉕ **accommodate**：適應、接受、容納

For this new model, Hans, we'll try to accommodate most of the fieldbus standards such as Profibus, Modbus, and CAN.

Hans，我們會在這新機種上納入多數 fieldbus 標準，像是 Profibus、Modbus、和 CAN。

㉖ **be concerned about**：對…擔心、憂慮、關心

Samantha, I'm concerned about the performance of your Marcom team.

Samantha，我對你們 Marcom 團隊的表現感到憂心。

㉗ **severe competition**：嚴峻、激烈的競爭

㉘ **run through**：指在電腦系統上跑過、測試過

Chris, did you run through our CRM to find the meeting minutes?

Chris，你有在 CRM 上找那份會議紀錄嗎？

NOTE

㉙follow rules：遵守規則

㉚magic word：關鍵字眼、神奇字眼

㉛investigate：檢視、研究、探究

Alex, we'll further investigate the case to see if we can accommodate your requirement.

Alex，我們會再深入研究這案子，看看能否將你們的需求也納入設計。

㉜take your time：慢慢來，不急

Janet, no rush and take your time.

Janet，不急，妳慢慢來。

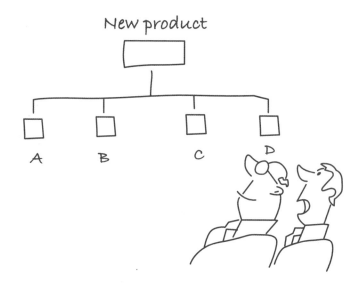

課文重點② **Summary 2**

For a B2B marketing person, new product planning has become <u>too vital to ignore</u> in recent years. Industrial marketing people will have to work closely with the salespeople, product managers, and also R&D engineers in different stages to <u>ensure</u> the <u>effectiveness</u> of new product development. <u>Meanwhile</u>, more and more marketing people are also <u>engaged in</u> regular <u>product life cycle</u> evaluation. Similarly in practice, an <u>EOL</u> decision is also an outcome of a <u>joint effort</u> from sales and marketing people as well as R&D engineers.

近年來，B2B 行銷人員越來越重視新產品規劃的工作了。工業產品行銷人員已無法閉門造車，而必須在不同階段與業務人員、產品經理、以及研發工程師們密切合作，以確保新產品開發成效。在此同時，有更多 B2B 行銷人員參與產品生命週期（PLC）評估。在實務作法上，停產（EOL）也是所有行銷、業務、與工程部門共同運作的結果。

產品開發流程：a systematic way to succeed 5-2

> **Michael** : **Sales VP, Wise Precision (vendor, Taiwan)**：業務
> 副總（臺灣供應商）
>
> **Sam** : **Sales Manager, Reese Land (master distributor,**
> **U.S.A.)**：業務經理（美國總代理）
> **Video conference** 視訊會議

Michael：Hi Sam, it's about time to continue our discussion about new products. Are you ready now?

嗨 Sam，我們得繼續前次關於新產品的討論了，準備好了嗎？

Dr. Lee 解析

由於是視訊會議，Michael 詢問對方，與會人員與所需器材是否已經準備好。

Sam：Yes, Michael, we're ready. Please go ahead.

是的 Michael，我們準備好了，請開始吧。

Dr. Lee 解析

確認可以開始討論了。

Michael : OK, let's start with the <u>pending issues</u> that we are going to <u>tackle</u>. I believe you have already prepared the information needed for today's meeting. Now would every one of you please <u>refer to</u> the <u>meeting minutes</u> on the screen?

好。我們就從還有爭議的議題開始討論。我相信你們已經把今天開會要用的資料準備好了。現在請各位先來看看銀幕上所顯示的上次會議紀錄。

Dr. Lee 解析

先前在展會結束後，雙方已經針對新產品需求討論過。這次視訊會議，就從一些未決議題開始繼續討論。

Sam : Yes Michael, we're all set. Actually we have obtained all the information by talking direct to our target accounts. And they're very happy to see things are <u>moving</u>.

是的，Michael，我們都準備好了。實際上，我們這些資料，都是透過直接和目標客戶對話取得的。這些客戶都很高興我們在這方面持續有進展。

Dr. Lee 解析

代理商所提供有關於產品新需求的市場資訊，對於廠商行銷業務部非常重要。代理商表示，所有資訊都是由目標客戶直接提供，真實性高。

Michael：Yes, we need to discuss all these cases <u>one by one</u>. However before that, I'd like to show you the procedures of new product development within our organization. I believe it will help you understand our decisions better.

好，我們會逐一討論這些案子。不過在那之前，我得先向各位介紹我們新產品的開發流程。如此一來，我相信你們會更了解我們未來的決策。

Dr. Lee 解析

廠商如果能讓代理商深入了解新產品開發流程，對於雙方合作開發幫助很大。

Sam：Very good Michael, <u>the more</u> we know, <u>the better</u> we'll be able to communicate with customers.

很好啊 Michael。我們知道得愈多，和客戶溝通的效果就愈好。

Dr. Lee 解析

當然也能幫助代理商面對終端客戶。

Michael：OK, as you can see from this slide, before a <u>formal review meeting</u> is held, we marketing and sales teams will have to do a <u>thorough</u> <u>research and evaluation</u> and <u>come up with</u> a new product <u>proposition</u>.

好，各位可從這張投影片看出，在開正式評估會議之前，我們行銷及業務團隊必須做全面研究和評估後，才能提出新產品開

發提議。

Dr. Lee 解析

> 產品開發最終能否成案，大多由參與評估會議的各相關單位主
> 管，與最高營運階層進行評估審核後拍板。首先行銷業務單位
> 必須進行各項商業分析，並做成新產品提案。

Sam：I see. So actually we have <u>gone through</u> stage one, correct? I mean after finishing the NWO show in Las Vegas last Friday, we did send you the <u>preliminary</u> technical requirements of the new instruments for our target customers. Did you have a chance to review them yet?

了解。所以我們已經通過了第一階段了，對吧？我是說，在上週五拉斯維加斯的 NWO 展結束後，我們已針對目標客戶所需，提出新產品初步技術需求。你們看了嗎？

Dr. Lee 解析

> 通常代理商面對終端客戶訂單壓力，多會積極配合廠商要求，
> 並期待快速進展。

Michael：<u>Not yet</u>, Sam. However I've <u>called a meeting</u> to discuss it next week. Both marketing and sales heads will be attending. We need to first make sure the proposed new products are <u>commercially viable</u>.

還沒，Sam。不過我預定在下星期開會討論，行銷和業務部門

主管都會參加。我們首先得確定你們提案的商業可行性。

Dr. Lee 解析

然而廠商往往受限於開發資源或其他因素，導致開發進度不如客戶預期。這裡廠商業務主管也承諾會盡力推動。

Sam : It doesn't sound too good to us. Michael, we've spent a lot of time communicating with you about these requirements since the NWO show. You also spoke to some of our customers last week at our booth. I don't understand what you're waiting for. Our customers won't waste any time on us as they are also talking to our competitors at the same time. Frankly speaking, I'm very surprised that you haven't shown any progress yet.

聽起來對我們不太妙。Michael，從 NWO 展以來，我們花了很多時間和你討論這些需求，你自己上星期也曾在我們攤位裡和客戶談過，我不明白你們在等什麼。這些客人同時也在和我們的競爭對手談，他們不會浪費時間等我們的。坦白說，我很訝異你們到現在一點進展都沒有。

Dr. Lee 解析

代理商顯然對於廠商遲遲沒動作感到擔心，開始施加壓力。

Michael : Well Sam, I fully understand your position. However, we are currently having a rather long new project queue. I'm very

sorry for the slow progress but I promise you that we will
<u>conclude</u> the final review meeting by next Friday.

Sam，我完全理解你的立場。但目前我們有一長串新產品開發
專案，進展慢了些，我感到很抱歉。不過我答應你，在下週五
的評估會議裡就能定案。

Dr. Lee 解析

廠商業務主管解釋進度不如預期的原因，並提出具體開發時間
表。

Sam : OK, I guess we can <u>live with</u> that <u>timeline</u>. I really hope all
the proposed new products will be approved. We've spent
lots of time and effort following up with our customers on
both technical and commercial issues in recent weeks. Now
it's about time to <u>get a result</u>.

好吧，我可以接受那樣的進度，希望我們所有提案都能通過評
估。最近幾週我們花了好多時間和心力，和客戶一起解決許多
技術和商業方面的問題，現在應該要開花結果了。

Dr. Lee 解析

代理商見目的已達成，表示能接受廠商所提的進度，並再次強
調他們與客戶對於新產品的高度期待。

Michael : I <u>can't agree more</u> with you on this. And I appreciate you
guys' efforts in providing us with so much information. Our

M&S team will further calculate some important <u>indices</u> such as resources needed, <u>scale of investment</u>, <u>projected P&L</u>, and <u>ROI</u>. And then we'll be ready for the final review meeting.

Sam，這點我完全認同。感謝你們花費那麼大的精力，提供我們這麼多資訊。我們行銷業務團隊會進一步算出一些指標數據，像是專案所需資源、投資規模、損益預估、投資報酬率等等。再來就準備開最後評估會議了。

Dr. Lee 解析

行銷業務對產品開發專案要負實際業績責任。<u>因此，對於各項行銷業務指標的分析、評估、與計算，都得大膽假設，小心求證。</u>

Sam : It's tougher than we imagined, <u>being frank with you</u>. How do you feel about the chance of <u>getting</u> all our proposals <u>approved</u> in the end, just <u>for our information</u>?

老實說，這種審核方式比我想像的還要困難。你也說來做參考，我們這些提案到頭來全數通過的機會有多大？

Dr. Lee 解析

代理商顯得有些<u>擔心</u>最後審核結果。

Michael : <u>They are looking really good</u>, according to our preliminary calculation. All the data showed <u>promising</u> business results. I'm very optimistic about the final outcome. More importantly, we don't see any technical difficulty in designing or producing such new products.

根據我們初步估算，通過的機會很高。所有數據都顯示有賺頭，我對最後結果很樂觀。更重要的是，無論在新品設計或製造方面，我們不會有技術上的困難。

Dr. Lee 解析

業務主管表示，經過仔細評估，他對於提案保持樂觀。

Sam : Awesome! If all goes well, we'll be selling one dedicated instrument to each of the four target markets in the foreseeable future. And I believe it will put us in a much better position against our competitors. You know that we are currently stuck in the middle of nowhere.

太讚了！如果一切順利，在可見的未來，我們在每一個目標市場中，都有一款專屬機種可賣。相信到時候，我們的競爭力就強多了。你也曉得，我們現在是深陷泥沼動彈不得。

Dr. Lee 解析

代理商當然很期待有好結果，新產品總會帶來新業績與利潤。

Michael : Yes, it will be a great opportunity for us to enhance our influence in these markets. We are looking forward to an all-win outcome. I mean a win for both of us and the end-user customers.

對，那將會是個強化我們市場影響力的大好時機。我們很期待一個全贏的局面：你、我、和終端用戶都賺錢。

Dr. Lee 解析

從廠商的角度來看，推出新產品代表在目標市場競爭力提高。若能順利開發成功，將形成全贏局面。

Sam : Now we need to discuss the EOL of model U6500. We received the latest <u>e-News</u> only last Wednesday. And we were <u>shocked</u> to learn that you set the EOL date of U6500 in less than 6 months from now. This is not acceptable. We still have many project orders to be <u>fulfilled</u> in 9 to 18 months from now.

現在我們得談談 U6500 的停產（EOL）。我們上星期三才收到這期電子報，看到 U6500 會在不到半年內停產，真是嚇了一大跳。這我們完全無法接受，我們在未來 9 到 18 個月當中，還有好多訂單要出。

Dr. Lee 解析

相對於新產品開發，工業產品停產決定同樣很重要，事前必須經過仔細調查分析，謹慎行事。

Michael : What? We didn't receive any such request from our <u>channel partners</u> while doing the EOL survey two months ago. That's why we set the EOL date on that day.

什麼？二個月前停產調查時，我們沒收到任何代理商有年後交貨的需求啊！所以，我們才把停產日定在年底那一天。

Dr. Lee 解析

停產事關重大，影響層面廣，代理商也須負責把關。

 : It was because one of the lost <u>tender orders</u> <u>came alive</u> two weeks ago <u>as a consequence of</u> a business <u>dispute</u> between the original winner and the end customer. We received the <u>formal P.O.</u> already but detailed product specs were <u>yet to be decided</u>.

Sam

因為二星期前，有個標案由於原得標者和客戶之間有些生意糾紛，生意失而復得又回到我們手中。我們已經收到訂單，不過詳細規格還沒確定。

Dr. Lee 解析

尤其是標案訂單，若因停產無法順利履行出貨，會產生嚴重損失。

 : OK, <u>done business</u> like this is always welcome and must be fulfilled, especially <u>under such circumstances</u>. <u>For safety's sake</u>, I will be checking with each of our channel partners again later this week to make sure the new EOL date will accommodate all requests <u>without fail</u>.

Michael

那好，這種到手的生意永遠不嫌遲，特別是在這種情況下，一

定得接下來。為了安全起見，我這星期會再和各地總代理確認，新的停產日期一定得完全滿足你們的需求。

Dr. Lee 解析

工業產品停產預告期大多夠長，好讓中間商與終端客戶有足夠時間因應。

Sam：Good. We will also do the same with our existing U6500 users again. To be honest with you, we don't think it's a good move to phase out U6500 so early because it's a very mature product. It has been so durable and reliable that we hardly received any returns for repair and maintenance. U6500 is truly a very good instrument for process control.

好的。我們也會再和所有 U6500 的用戶確認一次。坦白說，我認為你們不應該這麼早淘汰 U6500，因為它是個非常成熟的產品，耐操又穩定可靠，我們幾乎沒有收過退回維修的案子。U6500 的確是非常好的製程控制儀錶。

Dr. Lee 解析

基於短期利益考量，代理商往往不太願意廠商將穩定的老產品淘汰。

Michael：I agree with you that it is indeed a good product, and it has been in use for such a long period of time. However because of its old design, component supply has become a serious problem for us. From time to time we ran into short supply problems. Meanwhile it has become less profitable as a result of higher manufacturing cost. I'm sure you realize that our new model E8000 was designed to replace U6500 with advanced features and functions and a lower manufacturing cost.

我也認為 U6500 確實是好產品，而且上市已經有好長一段時間了。然而，因為是早期的設計，零件供應就成了大問題，不時會發生缺料的情形。同時，由於製造成本偏高，導致 U6500 利潤也不如以往。我相信你們也明白，用來取代 U6500 的 E8000，性能和功能都先進許多，而且製造成本也比較低。

Dr. Lee 解析

淘汰老舊機種，往往是因為關鍵零組件供應日漸困難。加上無法維持經濟生產規模，導致利潤受損。同時競爭對手的新產品，也可能影響銷售量。

Sam : We're still trying to get more familiar with E8000 as it is so powerful in terms of resolution, sampling rate, and fieldbus protocols. Actually these are fairly new to us, sales in particular. I guess we need to gear up and shorten the transition as much as we can.

我們還在學著更熟悉 E8000，特別是在解析度、取樣速率、和 fieldbus 通訊協議方面的超強特性。實際上，這些對我們，特別是業務來說，都是新的東西。我們得加緊腳步，儘可能縮短這個轉換期才行。

Dr. Lee 解析

替代產品，往往由於先進產品技術與新穎特性及功能，迫使廠商與代理商投資員工教育訓練，以期縮短產品過渡期，避免影響整體銷售。

Michael : Besides U6500, there are a few more models to be phased out in the next couple of years. They are either technically out-dated or not selling over the past several years. After finishing the financial evaluation, we will come back to you with the market survey.

除了 U6500，在未來幾年裡，我們還會再淘汰一些機種。這些機種，要不是由於性能老舊，就是過去幾年一直賣不好。在完成財務評估之後，我們會再回頭請你們做市調。

Dr. Lee 解析

會考慮停產，主要還是基於利潤考量。廠商都會定期做整體評估。

Sam : OK, we'll see what we can do with the issue by then.

好，到時候我們再來看看需要做些什麼。

NOTE

① **too vital to ignore**：口語中，「too 形容詞 to 動詞」的句型時常會用到

整句意思是：太（過於）「形容詞」導致不可（無法）「動詞」。此句 too vital to ignore 是說太重要以致不能忽視。

Tina is too tired to talk.

Tina 累到沒力氣說話。

② **ensure**：確保

③ **effectiveness**：成效、效果、效用

注意 effectiveness 與 efficiency 的差異：effectiveness 指成效、效果程度，而 efficiency 是指效率，是否省時、省力。

④ **meanwhile**：同時、在那期間

也可說 at the same time 或 in the meantime。

We'll be working on the G5 instruments in the next couple of weeks. Meanwhile, we'll continue to do environmental testing with the VT880.

接下來兩週我們會繼續 G5 儀錶的開發，同時也會持續對 VT880 進行環境測試。

⑤ **engage in**：參與、從事

Both Shannon and I are engaged in Project Jupiter.

我和 Shannon 都參與了 Jupiter 專案。

⑥ **product life cycle**：產品生命週期

⑦ **evaluation**：評估、評價、評核

NOTE

⑧ **EOL**：停產、下市

End of Life 的縮寫。

Jonathan, please try to evaluate the EOL of our G1 instruments.

Jonathan，請試著去評估 G1 儀表的停產。

⑨ **joint effort**：共同的努力

⑩ **it's about time**：該是時候了

⑪ **please go ahead**：請進行、請開始

⑫ **pending issues**：未決議題、事件

Daniel, we need to deal with these pending issues first.

Daniel，我們得先處理這些未決的議題。

⑬ **tackle**：解決

Tom, I think EMI/RFI is the number 1 problem we have to tackle.

Tom，我認為 EMI/RFI 是我們得首先解決的問題。

⑭ **refer to**：注意、參考

Please refer to Wednesday's product meeting minutes about the timeline.

請注意看星期三產品會議紀錄裡的時間表。

⑮ **meeting minutes**：會議記錄

⑯ **screen**：螢幕、顯示幕

⑰ **move**：進行

Sandy, we're so excited to hear the project has been moving well.

Sandy，聽到案子進行順利，我們太興奮啦！

⑱ **one by one**：逐一、一個個來

⑲ **the more…the better**：越多…就越好…

學習 the more…the better 的句型。

The more you practice, the better you speak.

你練得越多，就說得越流利。

The more you like your work, the better you enjoy it.

你越喜歡你的工作，就越能享受工作。

⑳ **formal review meeting**：正式評估會議

㉑ **thorough**：詳細的、詳盡的、徹底的

Cindy, be sure to make a thorough check on your presentation stuff tonight.

Cindy，今晚務必仔細檢查妳的簡報資料。

㉒ **research and evaluation**：研究和評估

㉓ **come up with**：想出、提出

Jacob, please don't tell me you came up with nothing but this.

Jacob，請不要告訴我你只想出這些而已。

㉔ **proposition**：提案、提議

NOTE

㉕**go through**：經過、通過

㉖**preliminary**：初步的

Guys, the preliminary test result doesn't look good at all.

各位，初步測試結果很糟糕。

㉗**not yet**：還沒有、尚未

Don, we have not yet received response from SpaceZ.

Don，我們還沒收到任何來自 SpaceZ 的回應。

㉘**call a meeting**：召集會議

Ella, would you please call a budget meeting on Friday?

Ella，能麻煩妳召集星期五的預算會議嗎？

㉙**commercially viable**：商業上可行的

Mia, the project makes lots of sense and we all believe it will be commercially viable.

Mia，這專案很合理，我們都認為未來一定能商業化。

㉚**It doesn't sound too good to us.**：聽起來不太妙。

㉛**booth**：展位，指展場裡的攤位

㉜**frankly speaking**：老實說

㉝**progress**：進度、進展

NOTE

㉞ rather+形容詞：相當+形容詞，**rather noisy** 相當吵雜。

Watch out, Dennis! The jigs are rather hot.
Dennis 當心！那些治具很燙。

㉟ queue：隊伍

也可用 line。

㊱ conclude：結束、做總結

James concluded the meeting with a touching video.
James 以一段感人的短片結束會議。

㊲ live with：指接受、勉為其難接受之意

Paul, we can live with minor cosmetic defects but we never compromise on any accuracy flaws.
Paul，我們能夠接受些微的外觀缺陷，但絕不在精度瑕疵上妥協。

㊳ timeline：時間表

也可用 timetable。

㊴ get a result：取得、獲得結果

Alex, after all the talking, it's time for you to get a result. Get orders!
Alex，說了這麼多，該端出結果了吧！你得拿訂單回來啊！

㊵ can't agree more：再同意不過了、非常同意

NOTE

㊶M&S team：行銷業務團隊

Marketing & Sales team 的縮寫。

㊷indices：單數形是 **index**，指標

㊸scale of investment：投資規模

㊹projected P&L：預測（預估）的損益

Brian, when will you send me the projected P&L for G5?

Brian，你何時能把 G5 的預估損益傳給我？

㊺ROI：投資報酬率

Return On Investment 的縮寫。

㊻being frank with you：坦白說

㊼get…approved：使…被核准（通過）

Derrick, your team must gear up and get our G5 approved by OIML as early as possible.

Derrick，你的團隊得加緊腳步，盡早讓 G5 通過 OIML 認證。

㊽in the end：最後、終究

Although we succeeded with a design-in, we didn't get a design-win in the end.

雖然我們成功拿到開發案設計承認，最後卻沒贏得訂單。

NOTE

㊾ for our information：給我們做參考

在許多 e-mail 中，多以 FYI 代表 for your information，而以 FYR 代表 for your reference。廣義來說，其實都是只提供訊息做參考。不過 FYR 多半是提供有來源的訊息。

㊿ they are looking really good：狀況很好、情況樂觀

51 promising：有希望的、有前景的

Bob, the sales forecast doesn't look too promising.

Bob，業務預估看起來不太妙。

52 look forward to：期望、期待

Denise, I'm looking forward to meeting you next Monday.

Denise，我期待下週一和妳會面。

53 all-win outcome：全贏的結果

指三方都贏。win-win 或 both-win 是雙贏。

54 e-News：電子報、數位刊物

55 shock：驚嚇、震驚

We were shocked when we heard that we failed to obtain OIML R76 approval.

在聽聞沒通過 OIML R76 的認證當時，我們非常震驚。

56 fulfill：履行

指跑完訂單流程出貨。

NOTE

57 channel partner：通路夥伴

指代理商或經銷商。

58 tender order：標案訂單、得標所取得的訂單

59 come alive：復活、重生

指訂單失而復得。

Richard, do you think the Reese TCXO order that they canceled last week will come alive again?

Richard, 你想上星期 Reese 取消的那張 TCXO 訂單還有可能起死回生嗎？

60 as a consequence of：由於…的結果

也可說 as a result of。

61 dispute：糾紛、紛爭

The recent dispute about the service level between Hank Steel and Sun Machining has been settled.

Hank Steel 與 Sun Machining 之間最近有關服務水準的糾紛已經和解了。

62 formal P.O.：正式訂單

P.O. 為 Purchase Order 的縮寫。

63 yet to be decided：尚待決定、尚未決定

Ethan, the official model name of G5 is yet to be decided.

Ethan，G5 的正式型號還沒決定。

NOTE

64 done business：已成交的生意

Matt, is there any reason for you to spend so much time on the done business?

Matt，你有任何理由花那麼多時間在那些已成交的生意上嗎？

65 under such circumstances：在這種情況（環境）下

66 for safety's sake：基於安全考量、為了安全起見

William, we'd better cancel the experiment, for safety's sake.

William，為了安全起見，我們最好取消這項實驗。

67 without fail：絕對、一定

Joseph, the temperature chamber must be installed and tested by 7:00 tomorrow morning, without fail.

Joseph，溫度測試箱絕對要在明天早上 7:00 之前安裝測試完成。

68 good move：好棋，正確作法

69 phase out：淘汰

I'm sorry, Jason, G2 was phased out a couple of years ago.

對不起，Jason，G2 在兩年前就已經淘汰停產了。

70 mature：成熟的

反義字：不成熟的 immature；早熟的、過於倉促的 premature。

71 durable：耐用的、耐久的

NOTE

72 **reliable**：可靠的

Ace Plating is a truly reliable plating firm.
Ace Plating 的確是一家可靠的電鍍廠。

73 **return**：（名）退回、退貨

74 **repair and maintenance**：修理與保養，簡稱維修

75 **process control**：製程控制

76 **indeed**：確實、真的

Benny, the G5 we just demonstrated to you is indeed an excellent process controller.
Benny，我們剛剛示範操作給你看的 G5，確實是一臺很棒的製程控制器。

77 **in use**：在使用的

The CRM software now in use is a cloud-based, on-demand system。
現在正在使用的 CRM 軟體是一套雲端運作的托管型系統。

78 **from time to time**：不時、有時

79 **short supply**：供給不及、短缺

Titanium alloy has been in short supply since last year.
從去年開始鈦合金就一直缺料。

NOTE

(80) **replace**：取代、替代

Because of the incident, Michael is going to replace Jacob on the development team.

由於這事件，Michael 將取代 Jacob，加入開發團隊。

(81) **advanced features and functions**：先進特性與功能

advanced 先進的。

(82) **get more familiar with**：對…更熟悉

Ricky, being a new member, you need to get more familiar with the systems.

Ricky，由於你是新人，你得對各類系統更加熟悉才行。

(83) **resolution**：解析度

(84) **sampling rate**：取樣速率

(85) **fieldbus protocols**：**fieldbus** 通訊協議

(86) **gear up**：上檔，指加快速度

Andy, you're falling way behind. Gear up and move faster!

Andy，你遠遠落後了喔，趕緊加速追趕吧！

(87) **transition**：轉換期、過渡期

(88) **outdated**：老舊的、落伍的

ZM is still using the outdated machines to fabricate sensor elements.

ZM 還在使用落伍的加工機器生產感應器彈性體。

NOTE

89 market survey：市場調查

Christine, where's the market survey report you were supposed to complete by 10:00 this morning?

Christine，你原本要在今天早上 10:00 前完成的市場調查報告在哪兒？

Lesson 6

定價：競爭與利潤
Competitiveness & Profitability

 課文重點① **Summary 1**

Setting up an effective pricing strategy and executing it properly on a daily basis are vital to every business, especially in B2B mode. When a manufacturer deals with multiple channel partners, managing pricing can be very complicated. Competition among those channel partners, primarily relating to pricing issues, is inevitable. It is the manufacturer's responsibility to establish a set of ground rules for all parties to follow. Again, the STP plays an important role in preventing channel conflicts.

對 B2B 模式的企業來說，制定出能在日常業務運作上有效執行的價格策略，是一件極為重要的事。廠商若是採取多通路銷售策略，售價管理就更為複雜。通路夥伴彼此競爭，尤其是價格競爭，在所難免。廠商就得制定出周全可行的規則，好讓各代理商或經銷商有所遵循。防止自家通路商競爭最有效的方法就是 STP：市場區隔、目標鎖定、及產品定位的追蹤考核。

通路定價：pricing for channel 6-1

Bob
：**Marketing VP, ST Taiwan**：行銷副總，ST臺灣

Jason
：**GM, Rock Instruments, dealer of ST Taiwan in Australia.** 總經理，ST Taiwan 澳洲經銷商
Conference call 多方電話會議

Bob
：Hello everyone, welcome to this meeting. We're going to spend some time reviewing all the <u>pending</u> pricing issues we've had so far.

哈囉，大家好，歡迎來參加這個會議。我們得花點時間來檢討所有至今未決的價格議題。

Jason
：As one of your dealers, we are always facing <u>tremendous</u> pricing pressures from our customers and also from other channels. Some of them are quite common and we had <u>little</u> problem with them. But some are really <u>nasty</u> and actually <u>unnecessary</u>.

身為經銷商之一，我們隨時都會碰上來自客戶和其他經銷商的龐大價格壓力。有些價格壓力很平常，我們並不會覺得太難應付。但有些就非常棘手，而且我覺得根本沒必要。

Bob
：Would you please be more <u>specific</u>, particularly with those nasty pricing issues?

能請你更具體說明嗎？特別是對那些棘手的價格事件。

Jason: Very often, the other dealer started the price war. We must have a clear guideline to follow. Otherwise, none of us will make money.

比較常碰到的情況是，別家經銷商開啟價格戰，一定要有一套明確的準則讓大家來遵循才行。否則到頭來，沒有一家經銷商能賺到錢。

Bob: I thought we had a gentleman's agreement many years before. And I believe it is still good, isn't it?

我記得多年前，我們經銷商之間，曾經有過君子協議。我相信那君子協議依然有效吧？

Jason: I suggest that we review it now and take all the relevant factors into consideration before we proceed.

我建議我們來檢討這君子協議，把所有相關的因素都納進來討論後，再來進行往後的議題

Bob: Good point, so besides quoting practices, what else do you suggest that we consider?

好主意，除了報價作法之外，還有什麼是我們應該考慮的呢？

Jason: I suggest that we cover STP, namely, segmentation, targeting, and positioning. If all the channel partners stick with their respective STP, we'll have very little conflict.

我建議納入 STP：區隔、標定和定位。倘若每家經銷商都能以自身的 STP 為行動準則，我們就幾乎不會有任何衝突。

Bob: Yes, definitely, STP must be reviewed ahead of pricing.

沒錯，討論售價之前，必須先檢討 STP。

NOTE

❶set up：建立、設立

❷effective：有效的

❸execute：執行

Matt, in order to execute the program, you have to become more determined.

Mat，為了要執行這方案，你得變得更有決心才行。

❹vital：重要的

Profitability is more vital to us than sales revenues.

獲利對我們來說，比營收更重要。

❺multiple channel partners：多家通路夥伴，即採取複式代理或經銷的情況

❻primarily：主要的

Dan, it is primarily an application problem, not a design problem.

Dan，那主要是個應用問題，不是設計問題。

❼inevitable：不可避免的、必然會發生的

❽ground rules：遊戲規則、競技規則

❾STP：**Segmentation** 區隔、**Targeting** 標定、**Positioning** 定位

NOTE

⑩ **conflict**：衝突

I'm sorry Denise. I can't make it because of a conflict in my schedule.

抱歉，Denise，由於行程衝突，我沒法參加。

⑪ **pending**：未決的、未定案的

Lisa, we need to conclude all the pending return cases relating to Ace Metals as quickly as possible.

Lisa，我們得儘速決定如何處理 Ace Metals 的未決退貨案。

⑫ **tremendous**：極大的、巨大的

⑬ **little**：極少、幾乎沒有

In the past, we paid little attention to the quality of packing cartons.

之前我們極不重視包裝紙箱品質。

⑭ **nasty**：令人討厭的、骯髒的、惡劣的

The way that Jonathan spoke to Daniel was particulary bad. He was being nasty for no good reason.

Jonathan 對 Daniel 的說話方式特別不好，惡劣的毫無道理。

⑮ **unnecessary**：沒必要的、多餘的

Danny, as of now, any further words on the issue will be unnecessary.

Danny，此時此刻，任何解釋都是多餘了。

NOTE

⑯specific：明確的、具體的

Susan, you have to be more specific with this slide.

Susan，妳得更具體解釋這張投影片。

⑰price war：價格戰

⑱otherwise：否則、要不然

I'd better leave now, otherwise I'll miss the flight.

我現在得走了，不然我會趕不上飛機。

⑲gentleman's agreement：君子協議

⑳take…into consideration：將…列為考慮、考慮到

Since you brought the issue up, we will take it into consideration when we evaluate the case tomorrow.

既然你提起了這議題，明天我們在評估個案時會考慮的。

㉑proceed：進行、繼續

Olivia, you may proceed now.

Olivia，現在妳可以繼續了。

㉒besides：此外、除了…之外

㉓practice：做法

The cash-upfront practice has been in existence for many years.

款到發貨的作法已經實施很多年了。

24 definitely：當然地、肯定地

Benny, we definitely need your continuous support.

Benny，我們當然需要你們持續支持。

課文重點② Summary 2

Increasing prices is <u>hardly</u> an easy job for most B2B marketing and salespeople, especially in <u>a highly competitive environment</u>. But <u>more often than not</u>, it is a must-do task as a <u>consequence</u> of <u>worsening</u> profitability. <u>Under such circumstances</u>, it is the responsibility of the salespeople to execute the program. It takes <u>a great deal of</u> <u>determination</u> and <u>persistence</u> to accomplish the mission. In practice, the most <u>challenging</u> task is to raise the <u>ASP</u> <u>on one hand</u> and avoid losing <u>voluminous</u> business <u>on the other</u>.

漲價對一位 B2B 行銷業務人員來說，永遠是一件難事，尤其是在一個高度競爭的環境裡更不容易。然而執行漲價卻一直是業務人員的天職之一。漲價是否成功，決心與堅持扮演極重要角色。在實際操作上，最困難的是既得成功漲價拉高 ASP，又得確保大訂單不流失。

全面漲價：General Rate Increase(GRI) 6-2

> **Steven**：**Marketing & Sales VP, Wise Precision (<u>headquarters</u>, U.S.A.)**：行銷業務副總，美國總部
>
> **Daniel**：**Sales Manager, Wise Precision (Taiwan <u>branch</u>, Taipei)**：業務經理，臺灣分公司，臺北
>
> **<u>Con-call</u> 多方電話會議**

Steven：Good morning, Daniel. <u>How's it going</u> with your team?

Daniel，早，你們團隊情況如何？

上司關心下屬團隊。

Daniel：Not very well, Steven. Competition, especially from those Chinese firms, has been <u>driving us crazy</u>. And now you told us there would be a <u>price hike</u>. I'm expecting strong <u>resistance</u> from the customers.

不怎麼好，Steven。特別是來自中國廠商的競爭，快把我們搞瘋了。現在你又來告訴我們得漲價，我估計客戶阻力會很大。

Dr. Lee 解析

競爭激烈環境下，又碰上得漲價，是業務最感焦慮的。

Steven：Take it easy, Daniel. <u>Never will</u> a price increase be easy, but we don't have to worry too much. I'm going to let you guys know the background of this general price increase before we start our discussion, so that you may have a better understanding of our decision.

放輕鬆些，Daniel。漲價一定困難重重，不過不用太擔心。在開始討論之前，我要說明一下這次全面漲價的原因，好讓你們能更了解我們的決策。

Dr. Lee 解析

老闆還是先安慰稍安勿躁，再進一步說明漲價的原因。

Daniel：Thanks. I'll be listening and hope it will help me calm our guys as they have been under <u>tremendous</u> pressure. I believe <u>the more</u> they understand the whole picture, <u>the better</u> they will do the job.

謝謝你，我將洗耳恭聽，希望能幫助我安撫手下業務，因為他們壓力確實很大。我相信如果他們對漲價原因了解多一些，他們的表現也會更好些。

Dr. Lee 解析

若能充分溝通，讓業務團隊了解實情，對於漲價的推動以及工作壓力紓解大有幫助。

Steven : Firstly, we need to <u>look into</u> the <u>P&L</u> of our division in the last 5 years. You can see from this slide that net profit has continuously been on a <u>downward trend</u>. Actually, we were <u>on the brink of</u> a loss last year. <u>From an operating point of view</u>, it is totally unacceptable. We don't have any <u>alternatives</u> other than execute a price increase. It has to be done <u>right away</u>, otherwise <u>we'll be in deep trouble</u>.

先來看看過去 5 年間，我們事業體的損益情形。你們從這張投影片可看出，整個事業體淨利呈現持續下滑的趨勢。實際上，去年我們已來到虧損邊緣了。從營運的角度來看，我完全不能接受這結果。除了實施全面性調漲售價，我們別無選擇。而且還得馬上行動，不然我們會有大麻煩

Dr. Lee 解析

漲價的壓力多半是由於獲利持續降低，甚至面臨虧損所引起。也因此，通常漲價都是緊急狀況。

Daniel : It sounds really serious. I checked with our financial manager <u>the other day</u> about our <u>financial performance</u> so far this year. She said it didn't look too <u>bright</u>, but we were still profitable. Now, from what you showed to us, it is <u>a different story</u>.

聽起來確實很嚴重。先前我詢問過財務經理我們今年以來的財務績效，她表示不太樂觀，不過還是有賺錢。現在聽你一說，發現並不盡然

Dr. Lee 解析

往往分公司的營收與獲利，和總公司必須看整體指標情形有差異。因此充分溝通是有必要的。

Steven : Well, Taiwan has been quite OK in terms of sales volume as well as operating profits. However when we take inventory into consideration, we found the profits decreased sharply as a result of much higher operating costs. Same happened to some other countries such as China, U.K., U.S.A., and Israel.

是啦，就營收與獲利情形來看，臺灣還算不錯。不過，如果把庫存也考慮進來的話，我們營運成本就明顯提高，導致獲利大減。相同情形也發生在其他國家，如中國、英國、美國、和以色列。

Dr. Lee 解析

庫存水準，往往是決定營運成本的重要項目之一。業務單位為了因應客戶的短單，經常要求多備庫存，也會造成獲利降低。

Daniel : So it will be an across-the-board price increase? It will apply to every item, every model, and every customer, correct?

所以這會是一次全面性漲價囉？會擴及到每一品項、每一型

號、和每家客戶，對吧？

Dr. Lee 解析

全面調漲影響層面很廣，業務的壓力會更大。

Steven : Basically, yes. We've worked out a price matrix for your quick reference. As you can see from the spreadsheet, for each item, each of our models, the selling price varies in accordance with the class of the customer. Headquarters marketing will be classifying all our customers into four categories, namely, category 1, 2, 3, and 4, based on the contribution of the particular customer over the past 24 months.

基本上是如此。我們已做好一份價格矩陣表，方便你們參考。從這份試算表裡可看出，每一品項、每一型號的售價，會隨著客戶等級不同而有所差異。而總公司行銷部門會依據客戶在過去 24 個月間對我們的貢獻度大小，把客戶歸成 1 至 4 級。

Dr. Lee 解析

全面漲價的實施機制，還是會根據商業買賣的慣性運作，將客戶以重要程度分等級，配合買賣規模制定新售價。一份完整的價格矩陣表，確實能在日常作業上，幫助業務人員進行價格訂正。

Daniel : Excuse me. You mean we need to adjust all our existing selling prices according to this price matrix? I could foresee resistance from our customers, as they will definitely be <u>con-fused</u> by the sudden price changes.

抱歉，你是說我們得根據這份價格矩陣表來調整現今所有售價？我能預見客戶絕對會反彈，因為我們突然更改售價勢必把他們弄得手忙腳亂。

Dr. Lee 解析

臨時通知漲價，確實會造成客戶的困擾與不便。因此業務人員會擔心客戶反彈。

: I understand, but <u>since</u> we have to do it <u>anyway</u>, it's better to let them know now.

Steven

我了解。但是既然我們遲早都得做，還是現在就告訴客人比較好。

Dr. Lee 解析

但嚴峻的情勢，讓上層無從選擇，勢必得漲價。

: The price matrix shows the increase exceeds 20% for almost all of our <u>hot-selling items</u>. I have to say that <u>in practice</u>, it definitely will be a lot tougher than you expect. I'm afraid that we'll be losing business very soon.

Daniel

由價格矩陣表看出，幾乎所有熱賣品項的漲幅都超過 20%。我必須說，實際執行起來肯定要比你預期的還要困難許多。我擔

心很快我們就要丟單了。

Dr. Lee 解析

對於大宗貨產品，客戶的價格敏感度極高。過大的漲幅，確實
會產生丟單的風險。

Steven : You haven't <u>even</u> tried. How do you know you'll lose business? I believe it won't be easy, however this is what we salespeople are supposed to do. We need to <u>implement</u> it <u>right away</u> and I'm <u>counting on</u> you to <u>accomplish</u> the task. It will <u>become effective</u> on October 1st, that is, three weeks from now. You'll be receiving the official price matrix later today.

你們連試都沒試，又怎麼知道一定會丟單呢？我也相信漲價不
容易，然而那本來就是我們業務人員的工作。我們得馬上採取
行動，而我得仰賴你來完成這任務。漲價是從十月一日就生效，
也就是三星期以後。今天稍晚你就會收到正式的價格矩陣表了。

Dr. Lee 解析

全面性調漲價格，高層的堅持與溝通是成功不二法門。各地區
業務經理也必須確實貫徹執行才行。

Daniel : Got it. I'll be working with my team members <u>in no time</u> to prepare for the price increase. Fortunately, we still have some time to work with the customers. I will come to you with the tough cases, if any, for help.

了解。我馬上會和業務團隊開始行動，幸好還有一些時間和客戶溝通。如果碰到難搞的個案，我會回頭請你幫忙。

Dr. Lee 解析

踏出第一步與客戶逐一溝通是關鍵。在此同時，業務經理也得協助手下業務人員保持適度彈性，有效因應客戶的疑慮及反彈。

: Yes, please do. This is exactly what I <u>was about to</u> tell you. Indeed we are determined to <u>make it a success</u>. Meanwhile, I want you to make sure we don't lose business. If you run into any <u>tough cases</u>, just come to me and I'll do everything possible to help.

Steven

是的，請務必要告訴我，正要告訴你這點。沒錯，我們有決心要漲價成功，同時我們也一定不能丟單。一旦你們遇上難搞的案子，儘管來找我，我一定盡力協助。

Dr. Lee 解析

成功調價的同時，也不容許因漲價而丟單。這得靠公司內部有效溝通協調，過程可能費時，不過只要下定決心，並保持彈性，成功機率還是很高的。

: Thanks very much. We would expect an <u>immediate</u> problem with model 8410 as it is actually a <u>commodity item</u>. If we increase our price by 5%, customers will definitely <u>switch to</u>

Daniel

competitors, <u>let alone</u> 20%. The same applies to model 3022, and I believe China and Israel will have a similar problem.

謝謝，大宗的 8410 馬上就會有問題。我們只要漲 5%，客戶會立即轉向別家買，就別說漲 20% 了。型號 3022 也一樣。我相信類似情形也會發生在中國和以色列市場。

Dr. Lee 解析

> 對於最有可能遭客戶反彈而丟單的大宗貨產品，業務經理在定案前再次發出警訊，不厭其煩地溝通。

Steven : I got your point. We will have to come up with solutions to this, I agree. For these three markets, competition is extremely fierce. Both George and David brought the issue up yesterday. Most likely, we will give special discount to <u>voluminous</u> orders <u>on a case by case basis</u>. I will <u>keep you posted</u> about my decision.

我懂你的意思。沒錯，我們得設法解決這問題。在這三個市場競爭特別激烈，George 和 David 昨天也都提出這問題。最可能的方式，就是予以個案處理，就是針對量大的訂單給予特別折扣。一旦決定，會通知你。

Dr. Lee 解析

> 顯然這已經是各地共通的問題，總公司高層自然會個案處理。

Daniel: OK, I'm somewhat <u>relieved</u> now. If we can deal with these two models properly, I'm quite confident that we will succeed in the end. By the way, Steven, will you also provide us with the revised <u>MSP</u> and <u>ASP</u> of each item? It will help us while negotiating with the customers.

好的，我現在鬆了一口氣。如果我們能順利解決這二項產品的問題，我有信心到頭來漲價會成功。對了，Steven，你還會提供我們各品項修正版 MSP 和 ASP 數據嗎？那對我們和客戶商談時很有幫助。

Dr. Lee 解析

> 有了共識之後，地區業務主管自然也能比較安心放手推動。實務上，MSP 與 ASP 是業務人員執行漲價最常用的資料。

Steven: I'm glad that you feel more comfortable now. Regarding MSP and ASP, yes, they will be included in the final price matrix. I really hope you don't <u>quote</u> MSP too often. And if we get closer to ASP, the overall financial status of the division will become much healthier.

很高興你現在覺得輕鬆點了。沒錯，MSP 和 ASP 都會併入最終版的價格矩陣表裡。希望你們不要經常用到 MSP，如果我們的售價能更接近 ASP 水準，整個集團的財務狀況就會變得更健康了。

Dr. Lee 解析

> 尤其是 ASP，它是決定公司是否獲利的最關鍵變數。而 MSP
> 只是在面對特殊需求時，用來參考的數據。

Daniel

: One more thing, Steven. It's about classifying customers.
I'd suggest that in addition to using sales performance in the
past 24 months as a basic criterion, marketing will take new
business prospects into consideration. The market changes
quickly, and we need to be flexible enough to accommodate
constant changes in the market.

Steven，還有一件事，就是有關客戶分級。我建議除了將過去
二年的銷售業績作為考量基準外，行銷部門也能一併把新客戶
發展性也納入考慮。市場瞬息萬變，我們得保持足夠彈性來因
應即時的變化。

Dr. Lee 解析

> 當然客戶的分級也是業務人員高度關切的，總希望行銷單位能
> 在現有業績表現之外，讓業務保持多點彈性。

Steven

: Daniel, we hope to keep the program as simple as possible.
Too many variables will make it too complicated to handle.
But if you run into any problem, please feel free to talk to
me, OK?

Daniel，我們希望漲價方案越簡單越好，過多的變數，會讓整
個方案太過複雜難以施行。但是你只要碰到問題，就儘管來找
我，好嗎？

Dr. Lee 解析

高層想法是先執行再說，沒必要顧慮太多，一旦遇到難題，再個案解決。

Daniel：OK, that's fine. Thanks.
好，沒問題。謝謝。

Steven：All right! Now let's get it done.
好，我們來搞定！

NOTE

❶**hardly**：幾乎不、幾乎沒

We hardly ever encountered any malfunctions with our high resolution instruments in the past 5 years.
過去 5 年間，我們的高解析儀器幾乎不曾發生故障。

❷**a highly competitive environment**：一個高度競爭的環境

❸**more often than not**：經常、通常、多半

More often than not, the customers come to us for help whenever they run into application trouble.
只要客戶碰到應用麻煩，他們通常會來找我們幫忙。

❹**consequence**：結果、後果

❺**worsening**：惡化中

NOTE

6 under such circumstances：在這情況下

Under such circumstances, we are forced to match their offer.

在這情況下，我們也只好跟進他們所報的條件。

7 a great deal of：大量的、許多的

8 determination：決心

9 persistence：堅持

Both determination and persistence are essential to the success of the price increase.

決心與堅持都是漲價成功的必要條件。

10 challenging：具挑戰性的

11 ASP：平均售價

為 *Average Selling Price* 的縮寫。

12 on one hand…on the other：一方面…另一方面

Simply put, we need to raise the ASP on one hand and keep our customer base intact on the other.

簡單來說，我們一方面得提高平均售價，另一方面還得不丢掉任何客戶。

13 voluminous：大的

Immediately, we lost a few voluminous orders to competitors as a result of the price increase.

由於漲價的結果，我們立即丢了幾張大訂單給競爭對手。

NOTE

⑭ **headquarters**：總部

多以複數形表示。

⑮ **branch**：分支機構、分公司

⑯ **con-call**：多方電話會議

conference call 的縮寫。

Tina, please schedule a con-call tomorrow afternoon with the PM and R&D teams.

Tina，請安排明天下午與產品經理和研發團隊的電話會議。

⑰ **how's it going?**：你好嗎？

非常口語的說法。

⑱ **drive us crazy**：把我們逼瘋、讓我們抓狂

⑲ **price hike**：漲價

⑳ **resistance**：阻力、反彈

The sudden price hike results in tremendous resistance from the customers.

這突如其來的漲價引起客戶極大的反彈。

㉑ **take it easy**：放輕鬆些、別緊張

㉒ **Never will**：注意以 **Never** 為句首的用法，助動詞得放在主詞之前。

Never will we leave our buddies behind.

我們絕不會棄同袍不顧。

NOTE

㉓ **tremendous**：極大的、巨大的

㉔ **the more…the better**：越…越好

The more you practice, the better you speak.

你練得越多，就說得越流利。

㉕ **look into**：調查、研究

Barbara, we'll look into the case as quickly as possible.

Barbara，我們會儘快調查這個案。

㉖ **P&L**：損益、盈虧

Profit & Loss 的縮寫。

Each BU has its own P&L to worry about.

每個事業體各有自家的盈虧得操心。

㉗ **downward trend**：下滑、向下走的趨勢

Jerry, I'm concerned about the downward trend of our ASP.

Jerry，我很擔心我們 ASP 下滑的趨勢。

㉘ **on the brink of**：瀕於、在…邊緣

Team, we need to make changes immediately as we're on the brink of losing money for the first time.

各位！由於公司正處於前所未見的虧本邊緣，我們得馬上做出改變。

㉙ **from an operating point of view**：從營運觀點來看

NOTE

㉚**alternatives**：替代方案

㉛**right away**：立即、立刻

㉜**we'll be in deep trouble**：我們將深陷大麻煩

㉝**the other day**：前些日子、日前

Mark, you told me the other day that the issue had been resolved.

Mark，你那天告訴我問題已經解決了。

㉞**financial performance**：財務績效，多半指營收與獲利

㉟**bright**：明亮、光亮

這裡是指業績表現良好的意思。

㊱**a different story**：不同的情形，另一回事

To deliver a convincing sales pitch isn't too hard. To close a deal is a different story.

要講一套有說服力的業務話術並不難，要拍板成交又是另一回事了。

㊲**take inventory into consideration**：考慮庫存水準

㊳**as a result of**：由於

Many people died as a result of the prolonged high temperature.

由於持續高溫，導致多人死亡。

NOTE

㊴ **same**：是指「相同情況」"same situation"

㊵ **across-the-board**：全面的
Benny, you're right. It is an across-the-board price increase.
Benny，沒錯，是全面性漲價。

㊶ **apply to**：適用於
Mia, the new selling prices will be applied to the orders placed by your company after December 1st.
Mia，新售價適用於貴公司在 12 月 1 日以後的訂單。

㊷ **quick reference**：快速參考，指方便參考
Hans, I'm sending this cost matrix for your quick reference.
Hans，我傳這份成本表方便你參考。

㊸ **spreadsheet**：試算表、試算底稿

㊹ **in accordance with**：根據、與…一致
We started to fight back in accordance with the conclusions reached in the latest sales meeting.
根據上次業務會議的結論，我們開始反擊。

㊺ **category**：類別、範疇

㊻ **contribution**：貢獻，指銷貨收入減去銷貨成本的部份

NOTE

47 foresee：預見

We foresee a quick recovery from the current slow-moving economy.

我們預見目前低迷經濟景氣將快速恢復。

48 confuse：使困惑

Not only did you fail to convince me, but you also confused me.

你不但沒能說服我，還讓我腦袋一片混亂。

49 since：既然、由於

Since you've made the final decision, we will comply with the guideline accordingly.

既然你已做最後決定，我們就會依照指示去做。

50 anyway：無論如何

Frank, I'll give you my final decision tonight anyway.

Frank，無論如何，我今晚會給你最後決定。

51 hot-selling items：熱賣商品

52 in practice：實際上、實施起來

In practice, it's a lot harder.

實際做起來，困難多了。

53 even：甚至

注意：even 在否定句中，是緊跟著助動詞之後。

I don't even know you.

我甚至都還不認識你。

NOTE

54 implement：實施

Team, we'll officially implement our CRM system in two weeks.

各位，我們將在二週內正式使用 CRM 系統。

55 right away：立即、即刻

56 count on：依賴、依靠

Barry, I'll have to count on you to lead the team.

Barry，我得靠你來領導團隊。

57 accomplish：達成、完成

Hey guys, mission accomplished. Congratulations!

各位，任務達成！恭喜啦！

58 become effective：生效

Alex, the new selling prices will become effective on January 1st.

Alex，新售價將從 1 月 1 日起生效。

59 in no time：立刻、馬上

Jimmy, I'll do it in no time.

Jimmy，我馬上去做。

60 be about to：即將

Manny was about to hit the road when he was told that his flight had been canceled.

Manny 才正準備要上路，就被告知航班已取消。

NOTE

61 make it a success：使成功、成功完成一件事

Vincent, you'll make it a success eventually, with all your hard work over such a long period of time.

Vincent，你長時間以來這麼認真工作，最終肯定會成功的。

62 tough case：很難搞定的個案

63 immediate：立即的

Michael, you have an immediate problem to solve, which is your poor performance.

Michael，你眼前有個立即得解決的問題，就是你那難看的業績。

64 commodity item：交易量大的商品、大宗商品

Nick, since 8410 is a commodity item, we have to match the lowest price to secure the order.

Nick，由於 8410 是大宗商品，我們必需跟進同行的最低價，才能拿下訂單。

65 switch：轉向、轉變

As a consequence of our insufficient capacity, the customer switched to our competitors.

我們產能不足，導致客戶轉向競爭對手下單。

66 let alone：更別提了、更不用說了

We won't even win with our MSP, let alone with any higher one.

即便我們用 MSP 都沒法拿到訂單，就別說用較高售價了。

NOTE

67 voluminous：大量的

68 on a case by case basis：視個案而定、個案處理

Guys, headquarters will consider our requests on a case by case basis.

各位，總公司會以個案方式考慮我們的要求。

69 keep you posted：隨時告知、一有消息立即通知

No problem, Andy. I'll keep you posted.

沒問題，Andy。一有消息就會通知你。

70 relieved：解脫的、心安的

Nancy was so relieved after knowing we won the order.

在得知我們贏得訂單後，Nancy 大大解脫了。

71 MSP：最低售價

Minimum Selling Price 的縮寫。

72 ASP：平均售價

Average Selling Price 的縮寫。

73 quote：報價

74 in addition to：除…之外

Mike, in addition to the monthly report, you'll have to hand in your Q2 B/B report by 5:30 p.m. today.

Mike，除了月報之外，你在今天下午 5:30 前還得交第二季的接單出貨比報告。

NOTE

㉟criterion：（評判）標準

複數為 criteria。

New customer development is one of the criteria we use to evaluate sales performance.

新客戶開發是我們用來評量業績的標準之一。

㊆flexible：有彈性的

㊆accommodate：容納、適應

Nancy, we definitely will do our utmost to accommodate as many of your requirements as possible.

Nancy，我們肯定會盡最大努力來接納你更多的要求。

㊆as simple as possible：盡可能簡單

Lisa, please keep your presentation as simple as possible.

Lisa，請你盡可能把簡報做簡單點。

㊆complicated：複雜的

Lesson 7 通路建立與夥伴關係
Channel Building & Relationships

課文重點① **Summary 1**

While marketing through <u>multiple</u> dealers in one particular region, it is very important for the marketers to <u>optimize</u> the <u>product offering</u> among these <u>channel partners</u>. It is indeed a difficult task as competition among <u>channel partners</u> <u>seems</u> <u>unavoidable</u>. Therefore, <u>it takes a ton of effort</u> to communicate with them <u>in hopes of</u> coming up with a <u>compromised</u>, if not 100% satisfactory, solution.

企業若是採同地區內複式代理或經銷模式的話，如何依據各通路夥伴在特定市場區隔裡的重點功能，規劃最適當產品組合，是行銷業務主管最重要，也是最困難的工作之一。主要原因是各通路夥伴彼此難以避免的同業競爭。特別是若有新通路夥伴加入時，往往利益衝突會更明顯。這都得透過事前周詳思考，加上耐心地溝通協調，以整體利益為優先考量。當然也得盡可能滿足各通路夥伴的需求。實務上，多方妥協後的方案，最有可能成為共識。

通路管理：channel management 7-1

> **Brenda**：**Marketing Manager, Lexton Systems (Taiwan)**：
> 行銷經理，臺灣
>
> **Michael**：**Sales VP, Tendon Distribution (Australia).** 行銷副
> 總，澳洲
>
> **Video conference** 視訊會議

Brenda：Hi Michael, very nice to see you. So glad we finally have a chance to see each other and work out a platform for future co-operation.

嗨 Michael，幸會幸會。很高興我們終於能會面，共同腦力激盪出未來的合作平臺。

Michael：Nice to see you too. We are also expecting good results after we complete reviewing the agreement drafts in detail.

很高興和您見面。也期待在詳細討論過合約草案細節後能有好結果。

Brenda：OK, let's start with the product lines that you proposed to carry and the territory you're going to represent.

好吧，就從你們所提議的產品線，以及你們想要代理的地區開始討論。

Michael：The territory is clear and easy to understand, but you can see we are way apart concerning the product lines to carry.

地區倒是很清楚也容易理解。但是你應該能看出，我們在產品線上可說是南轅北轍。

Brenda : Well, we realize there will be certain competition, however we believe it's going to be <u>minor</u>.

這個嘛，我們難免會有某種程度的競爭。不過我們認為，那只是小小的衝突。

Michael : I'm sorry, I think you <u>completely</u> <u>missed the point</u>. <u>According to</u> your plan, we will be selling the wrong <u>product mix</u> to a market where we have been the leader for more than 10 years.

不好意思喔，我想妳完全沒說到重點。按照你們的計畫，我們將會賣一整組錯的產品組合，到一個我們在過去十年裡一直稱霸的市場裡。

Brenda : I understand your position, but we already have another dealer <u>taking care of</u> that <u>segment</u>. This is the best we could do to help you.

我了解你的立場，但是我們已有別家經銷商在負責那塊市場，我們已經盡最大力量來協助你了。

Michael : Well, that's not what we expected and we will have to <u>drop</u> the case if this is all that we can get from you.

那並不是我們所期待的，如果這些就是你們可以提供給我們的話，我們只好放棄這個合作案了。

Brenda : OK, let me <u>think it over</u> and come back to you tomorrow. There might be something we can do for a <u>win-win situation</u>.

這樣吧，我回去再想想看，明天回覆你。或許我們可以商討出一個雙贏的作法。

NOTE

❶multiple：多重的、多樣的

Many Japanese firms selling overseas often sell through multiple dealers.

許多日本廠商在海外市場利用複式經銷進行銷售。

❷optimize：最佳化、最優化

One of our long-term goals is to optimize the corporate marketing resources.

達成公司行銷資源最佳化，是我們長期的目標之一。

❸product offering：提供的產品組合

offering 是指廠商如何針對不同經銷商，「提供」不同產品組合，以利經銷商銷售。

❹channel partners：通路夥伴

指代理商或經銷商。

❺seem：似乎、看起來像、顯得

Wendy, it seems to me that Reese Land wasn't too happy about our recent rate increase.

Wendy，Reese Land 似乎對我們最近調價不太高興。

❻unavoidable：無法避免的、不可避免的

David, as a consequence of the increasing labor cost, a GRI is unavoidable.

David，由於人工成本增加，全面調價將無法避免。

GRI 為全面漲價 General Rate Increase 的縮寫。

NOTE

⑦ it takes a ton of effort：得花很大氣力

it takes…需要、花上。

It takes 40 minutes to get to the airport from the hotel.

從旅館到機場需要 40 分鐘。

a ton of effort 數以噸計的努力，代表很可觀的努力。A ton of 多用在口語。

Our G5 posting on Facebook received a ton of "Likes" in less than 24 hours.

我們在臉書發佈的 G5 貼文，在不到 24 小時內就收到成堆的讚。

⑧ in hopes of：希望能…

We implemented the GRI in hopes of improving our gross margin.

我們實施全面性漲價，希望能改善毛利率。

⑨ compromise：妥協、折衷

We came up with a compromised solution.

我們想出一個折衷的解決方法。

⑩ platform：平臺、月臺

無論是屬於資訊或網路的平臺，或是實體的月臺都可以用 platform。

⑪ co-operation：合作

⑫ review：檢討、回顧、評論

Nick is going to review the sales performance of each sales office starting Monday.

Nick 從星期一開始要檢討各分公司的業績。

NOTE

⑬ **draft**：草稿

⑭ **in detail**：詳細地

Becky, you need to explain that in detail.

Becky，妳得詳細解釋才行。

⑮ **propose**：提議、提案、建議

I'd propose postponing the trip to Seagate Singapore.

我提議延後拜訪新加坡的 Seagate。

⑯ **carry**：在此並不是攜帶的意思，而是指經銷商手中所「經銷」的產品線。

XYZ Computers is carrying a complete line of laptops including HP, Asus, Toshiba, Sony, Lenovo, and many others.

XYZ 電腦門市經銷各品牌筆電，包括 HP、華碩、東芝、Sony、聯想，及其他品牌。

⑰ **represent**：代理、代表

We've been representing Reese Land in Taiwan for 20 years.

20 多年來我們一直是 Reese Land 的臺灣代理。

⑱ **way apart**：相隔很遠、差異太大

Edward, the figures you just provided were way apart from what you had committed to achieve.

Edward，你剛剛提供的數字和你早先承諾要達成的數字相差很大。

NOTE

⑲ **minor**：輕微的、較小的

Allen, I found a minor scratch on the panel.

Allen，我在面板上發現一處小刮痕。

⑳ **completely**：完全地

㉑ **miss the point**：沒抓到重點

Jennifer, I guess you've completely missed the point.

Jennifer，我認為妳完完全全沒抓到重點。

㉒ **according to**：根據、依照

We'll be able to launch G5 on October 1st, according to our timeline.

根據我們進度表，G5 能在 10 月 1 日上市。

㉓ **product mix**：產品組合

㉔ **take care of**：照顧、照料

Process Specialist is taking care of the factory automation segment for us in southern Taiwan.

Process Specialist 負責我們南臺灣工廠自動化區塊業務。

㉕ **segment**：區塊、區隔

㉖ **drop**：停止、丟掉

Alex, I suggest that we drop the case, considering the slim margin.

Alex，考慮到只有那麼一點點利潤，我建議放棄這案子。

NOTE

㉗think it over：仔細考慮、考慮清楚

Mark, please think it over.

Mark，請仔細考慮清楚。

㉘win-win situation：雙贏局面

或說 both-win situation。

 **Summary 2**

For a marketing professional, channel management is always a challenging task. In a B2B scenario, developing overseas markets in particular, manufacturers somehow run into channel conflicts. The master distributor has a different business focus from that of the manufacturer. As a consequence, some market segments are neglected and unattended. For example, the big OEM accounts that are used to dealing direct with manufacturers are not accessible easily by distributors because of both trade and non-trade obstacles. Consequently, very often the manufacturers will have to serve these customers directly. Under such circumstances, how do you manage the relationships with your distributors?

對一位 B2B 行銷人員，特別是針對國外市場的開發來說，通路管理一直是個很具挑戰性的任務，不時就會碰上通路衝突的難題。總代理與製造商的經營重心相去甚遠，導致常有部分市場區塊被忽略。舉例來說，習慣直接和廠商打交道的大型 OEM 客戶，由於貿易或非貿易障礙，總是讓代理商覺得難以接近。這樣下來，廠商往往得自行出面與這些「直接客戶」打交道。碰到這類狀況，到底該如何經營與代理商的關係呢？

通路與直接客戶：channel & direct accounts 7-2

> **Simon**：**Sales Manager, Wise Precision (Taiwan Head-quarters)**：業務經理，臺灣總公司
>
> **Sato**：**President, Kanto Sokki (Master Distributor, Ja-pan)**：社長，日本總代理
>
> **Simon is visiting. Simon 前去拜訪。**

Simon：Good morning, Mr. Sato. It <u>has been</u> more than six months <u>since</u> we met last time. <u>How's it going?</u>

早安，Sato 先生。距離我們上次見面已有半年了，你好嗎？

Dr. Lee 解析

顯然廠商業務主管 Simon 有定期拜訪代理商。

Sato：I'm fine, thank you. Yes, <u>time flies</u> but I still remember we had a nice meeting last time. I appreciate you coming to see us again. What's your <u>agenda</u> today?

很好啊，謝謝你。時間過得真快，我還記得上次我們見面談得很愉快。真謝謝你又來看我們，今天的議題是什麼呢？

Dr. Lee 解析

定期會面好處多，廠商與代理商都受惠。每次拜訪都應該有具體討論主題。

Simon :

It always feels good to come and meet you here at Kanto Sokki. I do have an important topic for the meeting this morning. It's about the huge business from some big equipment builders such as Yamato and Kubota.

每次來和各位見面都很開心，今天早上我們得討論一個重要議題，是有關於幾家大型設備廠客戶，像是 Yamato 和 Kubota 的大生意。

Dr. Lee 解析

中心討論議題很清楚，就是那塊 OEM/ODM 生意。

Sato :

We have discussed this issue many times before. Unless you're bringing along a new and effective solution, it's pointless for us to do it again today. Please bear in mind that we're a value-added system company, and such business doesn't fit in with our business model.

這個議題先前我們討論過好幾次了，除非你有帶來新的有效解決方案，不然今天再談這些其實沒什麼意義。請記住，我們是一家加值型系統公司，那種業務和我們的商業模式不合。

Dr. Lee 解析

顯然在此之前雙方談過多次未能有共識，主因是獲利模式看法差異。

Simon : I know your point very well. And I don't mean to interfere with the way you run your business. Nevertheless, the OEM/ODM business is too important for us to give up without taking action. Since we don't have an office here in Japan, we need your direct assistance to develop the market.

我很清楚你的意思，也無意干涉你的經營方式。然而，OEM/ODM 生意對我們實在太重要，不可能眼睜睜地就此放手。因為在日本我們沒有銷售據點，我們需要你們直接幫忙開發這塊市場。

Dr. Lee 解析

廠商當然不會輕易放棄任何生意機會，更何況是如此大規模市場。至此還抱著一線希望現行代理商能同意合作，減少麻煩。

Sato : As I just said, you failed to show us how it will work for us with your previous proposals. Firstly you suggested that we resell to them. Apart from the pricing issue, there's one thing many foreign companies failed to understand. In Japan, the industrial measurement business is still a traditional industry. Customers like Yamato and Kubota would deal with the big Japanese trading firms like Mitsubishi, Mitsui, or Marubeni. This is the culture of Japan's traditional industries.

我說過，你們前幾次提案，我們認為行不通。起先你們還建議由我們轉售，要知道撇開價格因素，有一件事是許多外商無法了解的。在日本，工業量測行業依舊是個傳統產業。像 Yamato 和 Kubota 這種客戶，還是喜歡透過三菱、三井、或丸紅等大商社對外採購，這是日本傳統產業的文化。

Dr. Lee 解析

這種生意原本就不該屬於代理商，主要是利潤和一些非貿易門檻因素，如生意模式和售前售後服務。

Simon：That's news to me. Thanks very much. I guess those trading firms would take care of everything from finding and getting the needed products, delivering to the customer's warehouse, and providing all the services and support needed. And of course, they may offer attractive trading terms such as a longer payment period. I believe you may also do the same, right?

我第一次聽到這樣說法，感謝指教。我猜想，那些大貿易商從找貨、訂貨、交貨，到售後服務、技術支援都能全部搞定。當然他們也會開出很誘人的交易條件，例如較長的付款期。這些你們也做得到，對吧？

Dr. Lee 解析

日本大貿易商對某些產業依舊有其特有功能，廠商從而再試探代理商意願。

Sato : <u>Not exactly</u>. Although we are able to handle import and export business <u>without a problem</u>, we do it only <u>for our own benefit</u>. <u>Yet</u>, pure reselling will never become a <u>business model</u> of ours. Providing our customers with added value or a <u>total system solution</u> <u>has long been</u> the <u>core</u> of our business. To be more <u>practical and specific</u>, it will hurt our overall profitability to do pure <u>buy-and-resell</u> business with our current cost structure. I don't understand why you're still <u>insisting</u> we do it for you.

其實不盡然。雖然進出口對我們不是問題，但我們是為了自己的利益而為。純粹轉手買賣永遠不會成為我們的業務模式。我們的核心業務一直都是提供客戶附加價值，或是成套系統性解決方案。說得更實際更具體些，以我們現今的營運成本結構來看，單純做轉手買賣會危害到公司整體的獲利率。所以我實在不理解，為什麼你還那麼堅持要我們那麼做？

Dr. Lee 解析

代理商清楚再度表態，無意願進入純轉售模式，並強調加值才是他們核心生意，轉售只會稀釋加值所帶來的高利潤率。代理商也軟性抗議。

Simon : Please <u>don't get me wrong</u> <u>in this regard</u>. I fully understand your position. And that's why I'm bringing with me two <u>options</u> that we believe to be more <u>feasible</u> for us to work together in the future. The only <u>concern</u> we have so far is that we will have to <u>divide</u> the Japanese market <u>into</u> two segments, namely channel and direct. "<u>Channel</u>" means through a distributor like Kanto Sokki while "direct" means direct accounts like Yamato and Kubota.

關於這點請你不要誤會,我完全能理解你們的處境。所以這次我準備了二個方案,相信會大大增加我們未來合作的可行性。目前我們擔心的是,必須將日本市場分成「通路」和「直接客戶」二大區塊。「通路」就是像 Kanto Sokki 這樣的代理商,而「直接客戶」就是像 Yamato 和 Kubota 那樣的客戶。

Dr. Lee 解析

見機行事,廠商發覺阻力仍大,隨即頒出口袋方案,將 OEM/ODM 直接生意單獨分割出來。

Sato : I remember I made a similar recommendation to you early last year, when you visited us at the InterMeasure show in Tokyo. I'm glad you accepted my proposal. We don't mind if you deal directly with Yamato or Kubota for their business. I think they'll be glad to do business with you because you are an American company.

我還記得,去年初你來參觀我們在東京 InterMeasure 展時,我曾經當場向你提出類似的建議。很開心你接受我的提議,我完全不介意你們直接和 Yamato 及 Kubota 接觸談生意。因為你們是美商公司,我相信他們會很樂意和你們做生意的。

Dr. Lee 解析

代理商不甘示弱,也趁機邀功表示早就建議過。

Simon : Yes, that's how we planned to deal with the Japanese market as <u>a whole</u>. However, we <u>haven't yet</u> made our final decision on <u>whether</u> to <u>set up</u> our own sales office <u>or</u> to work with a new partner for direct business. Do you have any suggestions?

沒錯，那就是我們對於日本市場的整體計畫。不過，我們還沒決定是要在日本設立自己的銷售據點，還是找一家新的合作夥伴來拓展直接客戶生意。你有什麼建議嗎？

Dr. Lee 解析

在日本投資設立據點或是另外找合作夥伴都是選項，廠商不忘請教代理商。

Sato : Let me ask you one question first. Do you have any <u>candidates</u> for the new partner? Although we don't want to influence your decision, we are indeed concerned. The industry is so small that we need to make sure that our business is <u>secured</u>.

我先問你，這新通路夥伴你有人選了嗎？雖然我們無意影響你的決定，但我們還是很擔心。這行業太小了，我們得確保自己的生意不受到傷害。

Dr. Lee 解析

沒錯，代理商最在意的還是自身的利益。

Simon : OK, I'll tell you what I was <u>authorized</u> to disclose. Firstly, we will not invest in setting up our own office in Japan, at least <u>for the time being.</u> <u>Instead,</u> we're thinking of signing an agency agreement with Yokogawa Keiki of Yokohama for direct business. Are you <u>familiar with</u> Yokogawa Keiki?

好，我把能說的都告訴你。首先，我們不會投資設立日本銷售據點，至少暫時不會。不過我們正在考慮和橫濱的 Yokogawa Keiki 簽代理合約。你們和 Yokogawa Keiki 熟識嗎？

Dr. Lee 解析

廠商不直接投資在設立據點上，改以另尋代理，這也是原代理最擔心的。

Sato : Of course we are familiar with them. Actually their main factory is very close to us, only <u>15 minutes away from here.</u> And to tell you the truth, we have been competing with each other in a few market segments such as <u>process automation</u> and <u>unmanned parking systems.</u> We're surprised that you'd appoint them as your second agent in Japan without <u>checking with</u> us <u>beforehand.</u> I'm very disappointed in your decision as we've been working together for more than ten years.

當然很熟。實際上，他們的主要廠房就在附近，離這裡只有 15 分鐘遠。老實說，我們彼此在製程控制和無人停車系統市場裡是競爭對手。對於你們事先沒來詢問就選定他們作為第二家代理，我們感到很意外。我對你們這項決定感到很失望，畢竟我們都已經合作超過 10 年了。

Dr. Lee 解析

> 代理商自然明白同行競爭在所難免，何況是在同一地區。他們
> 在意的是廠商事先竟然沒照會，感覺沒面子，很多較保守日本
> 廠商會因這樣感到不好受。

Simon: Please try to understand our position in this case. It was a tough decision for us, but we can't afford to incur any further delay on this issue. Of course we realize that Yokogawa competes with you in a few markets, however we're not selling them any of our products for distribution. Instead, they are confined to OEM/ODM business only. As of now, there are only six customers with whom they are allowed to do business, and I believe none of them have been approached by you.

請你能了解我們的立場，做這樣決定很煎熬，不過我們在這事上已經不允許再拖延了。我們當然知道 Yokogawa 在一些市場上和你們競爭，不過我們不會賣任何產品給他們做轉售。他們只做 OEM/ODM 生意，現在僅僅能和 6 家客戶打交道，我相信你們不曾接觸過這些客戶。

Dr. Lee 解析

> 廠商也一再說明做此決定的必要性和困難度，並保證會對新通
> 路夥伴有所規範。

Sato: You're right that none of them has had any business with us.

What I care about is that, actually, we <u>are willing to</u> help you find a capable agent for direct business. And we did expect that you'd check with us regarding this. <u>After all</u>, we've been business partners for such a long time. Although we've <u>rejected</u> your previous business proposals, we'd still be glad to help you as a partner.

沒錯，我們和這些廠家之間沒有生意往來。我在意的是，其實我們很願意幫你找一家負責直接客戶的代理商，也期盼你會來詢問。畢竟我們是很久的生意夥伴了，雖然我們拒絕過你們之前的提案，身為相互信任的夥伴，我們還是很樂意幫忙的。

Dr. Lee 解析

原代理還是耿耿於懷，一再強調合作夥伴相互幫忙的心意。

Simon : Don't worry. I understand it, and <u>I appreciate it</u> very much. You are still one of our most important channel partners. And please <u>rest assured</u> that appointing Yokogawa as our second agent in Japan won't create any <u>conflict of interest</u> among us <u>nor</u> will it <u>do any harm</u> to the relationship between our two companies.

別擔心，我了解的，也很感謝。你們依舊是我們最重要的通路夥伴，請放心，即便選了 Yokogawa 作為第二家代理，也絕不會產生任何利益衝突，更不會傷害到我們之間的關係。

Dr. Lee 解析

> 廠商一再保證現有關係不受影響。事實上雙方都在安撫對方，
> 希望這事件能順利告一段落。

Sato : Thank you so much for your kind words. We also believe that it will not create too much competition with us <u>either</u>. We wish you luck in getting more direct business with their help. But we're still wondering how they can <u>sustain</u> such a low profitability <u>over the long run</u>. Do you mind telling us a little about this?

真謝謝你這番好話，我們也不認為那會帶來多少競爭。希望透過他們幫忙，你們能多做些直接客戶生意。不過還是很好奇，長久下來，他們如何能靠如此薄利存活，你介意透露多一點訊息嗎？

Dr. Lee 解析

> 合作不成仁義在，場面話還是得說。現有代理對於轉售生意獲
> 利感到好奇。

Simon : No problem at all. Basically, Yokogawa will be <u>working on a commission basis</u>. We'll be <u>exhibiting</u> at certain trade shows for certain products such as TH3220, BV3120, and CSP. All of them <u>fall into</u> the ODM category. I'm sorry that I can't disclose all the details, but it is a very <u>straightforward</u> cooperation.

沒問題。基本上，Yokogawa 只抽佣金。我們會和他們一起參

加幾場展會，推幾個 ODM 機種，像 TH3220、BV3120、和 CSP。抱歉，我無法透露更多細節。但真的只是很單純的合作而已。

Dr. Lee 解析

> 直接客戶生意新代理同意以抽佣金方式合作，而廠商將以共同參展方式協助新代理推展業務。

Sato : That's all right. Maybe we'll be able to see each other at the trade show. Anyway, if we can be of any service to you, please feel free to call us. I treat you not only as a business partner, but also a personal friend. You earned it over the years. Let's have a drink after the meeting, OK?

沒關係的，或許我們會在展會上見面也不一定。不管怎樣，如果我還能幫上什麼忙，請別客氣儘管打電話給我。你不但是我的生意夥伴，更是我私人朋友。這是你個人這幾年努力得來的。會議結束後我們喝一杯吧！

Dr. Lee 解析

> 畢竟生意關係得繼續維持，即便過程中現有代理有諸多不滿，還是得有所克制。

Simon : I'd love to. And thank you for being so frank and considerate to me. It always feels good to come and chat with you. Today is no exception.

樂意奉陪。非常謝謝你對我這麼坦誠體諒，每次來和你聊天都好開心，今天也不例外。

Dr. Lee 解析

會後喝一杯有助強化交情！

NOTE

❶**marketing professional**：專業行銷人員

❷**channel management**：通路管理

❸**challenging task**：挑戰性高的工作

❹**scenario**：情境、情景、情況

Ricky, the worst-case scenario will be that we lose this account.
Ricky，最糟糕的情況就是這客戶不保了。
the worst-case 最糟糕的。

❺**develop overseas market**：開發國外市場

❻**in particular**：特別是、尤其是

Paul, competition drove down our ASP on the 96 x 48 display in particular.
Paul，市場競爭壓低了我們的 ASP，尤其是 96 x 48 控制器。

NOTE

⑦ somehow：某種程度上

Benny, many of our customers are somehow not comfortable with our long lead time.

Benny，許多客戶對我們交期太長，感到某些程度的不安。

⑧ run into：碰上、遇到

Helen, if you run into any problem regarding pricing, make sure you come to me as quickly as possible.

Helen，如果你們碰到任何價格上的問題，請務必盡早來找我。

⑨ master distributor：總代理商

⑩ focus：聚焦、焦點

引申解釋為重點。

⑪ segments：區隔、區塊

Nathan, we need to focus on those market segments that are most profitable to us.

Nathan，我們得集中火力在那些高利潤市場區塊。

⑫ neglected：被忽視的

⑬ unattended：沒被注意的、沒被照顧的

Samuel, we shouldn't have neglected the power of web marketing and left the long-tail market unattended.

Samuel，我們實在不該輕忽網路行銷的威力，沒去照顧長尾市場。

NOTE

⑭ **for example**：舉例來說：例如

⑮ **be used to**：習慣、慣於

Ella, we are used to working overtime on Friday night.

Ella，我們已經習慣週五晚間加班。

be used to 後若接動詞時須以現在分詞呈現，如 we are used to working。

⑯ **accessible**：可以接近的、容易接近的

Lisa, we should make our online customer service more accessible to the customers.

Lisa，我們得讓客戶更容易連結到線上客服。

⑰ **trade and non-trade**：貿易的和非貿易的

⑱ **obstacle**：障礙、阻礙

⑲ **consequently**：所以、因此

Consequently, technological know-how becomes the entry barrier of the industry.

所以，專門技術就成為這產業的進入障礙。

⑳ **has been…since**：自…以來

表示期間的現在完成式，在口語中經常使用。has been 後接期間長短，而在 since 後則用過去的一個時間點。

Hi, Barbara, it has been over a year since you were transferred to the Singapore office.

嗨 Barbara，自從妳調到新加坡以來，都已經超過一年了。

Frank, it has been a long time since we last met in Sydney.

Frank，自從上次我們在雪梨相遇至今也好久了。

㉑ how's it going?：你好嗎、如何啊
非常口語的說法。

㉒ time flies：時光飛逝、時間過得真快

㉓ agenda：開會的議程

㉔ It always feels good：我很高興…
也是口語中常用的句型。It 代表 to 以後的動作，取代 I'm happy…。
It always feels good to be on the road visiting customers.
外出拜訪客戶總是讓我感到開心。

㉕ huge：龐大的、巨大的

㉖ equipment builder：設備製造廠

㉗ issue：事件、問題、爭議
Guys, we have an issue here.
各位，我們有個問題（或爭議）

㉘ bring along：帶著、帶來

㉙ pointless：沒有意義
It's pointless for us to meet up here if you don't have a plan with you.
如果你沒帶計畫來，我們在這見面就完全沒意義了。

㉚ bear in mind：記住、記在心裡
Bear in mind that Acer used to be one of our top-5 accounts.
記住，Acer 曾經是我們前五大客戶之一。

NOTE

㉛value-added：加值的

We're specialized in providing value-added service from system design to system installation and to commissioning.

我們的專業是提供由系統設計、系統安裝,到試運行的加值服務。

㉜fit in：適合、融入

Larry, the product that you are offering does not fit in with our kind of business.

Larry,你提供給我們的產品不適合我們的生意模式。

㉝business model：商業模式、企業模式

㉞I don't mean to⋯：我無意⋯

Jack, I don't mean to be critical, yet you've lost your focus completely.

Jack,不是我吹毛求疵,但是你完全失焦了。

㉟interfere with：干涉、干擾

Bob, I'm not going to interfere with the way you run your business.

Bob,我不干涉你經營公司的方法。

㊱nevertheless：儘管如此、然而

㊲OEM/ODM：是 Original Equipment Manufacturer / Original Design Manufacturer 的縮寫

NOTE

㊳ **give up**：放棄
Emma, hang in there. Don't give up.
Emma，撐住啊！別放棄！

㊴ **take action**：採取行動

㊵ **work for us**：（對我們）行得通、有利
Emily, show us how the project will work for us.
Emily，讓我們看看這專案對我們如何有利。

㊶ **resell**：轉售

㊷ **apart from**：除開、除了…之外
Apart from helping customers solve their application problems, we provide them with comprehensive technical training.
除了協助客戶解決應用問題之外，我們還提供他們完整的技術訓練。

㊸ **fail to**：沒能、未能

㊹ **traditional**：傳統的

㊺ **deal with**：交涉、交易、處理
Mia, you have to be much more patient while dealing with Japanese businessmen.
Mia，在和日本人做生意時，妳得更有耐心些。

㊻ **culture**：文化

NOTE

47 that's news to me：我不知道、我沒聽過

48 take care of everything：搞定一切、辦妥所有事情

Allen, you go get the order and we'll take care of everything else.

Allen，你儘管接單，其他交給我們搞定。

49 deliver：交貨

50 trading terms：交易條件

51 not exactly：不盡然、不完全是

Things are not exactly as Jeff mentioned.

實際情況並不完全像 Jeff 說的那樣。

52 without a problem：沒困難、不會有問題

53 for our own benefit：為了自己的利益

Anthony, we did all these for our own benefit.

Anthony，我們所有作為全是為了我們自己的利益。

54 yet：但是、然而

Daniel, we didn't get the business, yet each and every one of us learned.

Daniel，我們並沒拿到生意，但是我們每個人都學到東西。

55 business model：生意、商業模式、經營模式

56 total system solution：完整的系統解決方案

也可說 turn-key solution。

NOTE

㊄ have long been：早就是、長久以來都是

Selling total system solutions in the automation industry has long been our number one task.

長久以來，在自動化產業中提供完整的系統解決方案，一直是我們的首要工作。

㊄ core：核心

㊄ practical and specific：實際且具體

㊅ buy-and-resell：買進轉售、買進轉手賺差價

㊅ insist：堅持

Ryan, I am insisting on sending our quotation to Reese Land this morning.

Ryan，我堅持今天上午就傳報價單給 Reese Land.

㊅ don't get me wrong：不要誤會我、別搞錯

Loraine, please don't get me wrong. I wasn't trying to give anybody a hard time.

Loraine，請別搞錯，我並沒要為難任何人。

㊅ in this regard：在這方面、在這點上

㊅ option：選項、選擇

Susan, giving up is never an option for us.

Susan，對我們來說，放棄絕對不是選項。

NOTE

㊕feasible：可行的、適宜的

Ian, we need to review the situation carefully and see if it is feasible to offer special rates to Acer.

Ian，我們得仔細研究整個情況，以決定是否適合給 Acer 特別價格。

㊌concern：擔心、顧慮

㊍divide…into：分割成

Basically, we divide the frequency control devices into crystals and crystal oscillators.

基本上，我們將頻率控制裝置分割成石英振盪晶體和石英震盪器二大類。

㊎channel：是指「通路」生意，透過代理商或經銷商銷售的生意。

㊏direct：是指「直接客戶」生意。不經由代理商或經銷商銷售，而直接由廠商負責銷售的生意。

㊐recommendation：建議

㊑mind：介意、在意

Do you mind if I cancel our latest order?

倘若我取消最近那張訂單，你會在意嗎？

Dennis, we're in the meeting. Would you mind taking off your headset, please?

Dennis，我們正在會議中，你不介意把耳機拿下來吧！

⑰ as a whole：整體（考量）

Paul's team, as a whole, has been doing a great job.

整體來說，Paul 的團隊表現得很優秀。

⑱ haven't yet：還沒、尚未

現在完成式否定用法。

I'm so sorry, Olivia, we haven't approved your SR application yet。

真對不起，Olivia，我們還沒核准你們特別價格的申請。

Lynn, we haven't yet come up with a better solution.

Lynn，我們還沒想出一個更好的解決方法。

⑲ whether…or：是要…或者

It makes little difference whether we go or stay.

我們去或留下根本沒差別。

⑯ set up：設立、建立

⑰ candidate：候選人、候選對象

⑱ secured：安全的

Samuel, please make sure our position in the femtocell market is solid and secured.

Samuel，請務必確保我們在微型基地臺市場中地位安全穩固。

⑱ authorized：被授權的、被准許的

Terry wasn't authorized to sign on the SCM system.

Terry 並沒有被授權登入 SCM 系統。

NOTE

⑦ for the time being：目前、暫時

Ethan, we have enough stock, at least for the time being.
Ethan，至少目前我們有足夠的庫存。

⑧ instead：反而、反倒是

We didn't go picnicking. Instead, we went swimming.
我們沒去野餐，而是去游泳了。

⑧ familiar with：熟識、熟悉

⑧ 15 minutes away from here：距離這裡15分鐘路程

⑧ process automation：製程自動化

⑧ unmanned parking systems：無人管理停車系統

⑧ check with：這裡是指徵求 **Kanto Sokki** 對於挑選第二家代理的看法。

⑧ beforehand：事先、事前

⑧ tough decision：很困難的決定

⑧ can't afford to：承擔不起

We can't afford to make any more mistakes.
我們承擔不起再犯任何錯。

NOTE

89 be confined to：被限制在某一範

90 as of now：現今、當下

91 approach：接近
在此是指被 Kanto Sokki 聯繫過或談過生意的意思。

92 be willing to：願意、樂意

93 after all：畢竟、終究

94 reject：拒絕、回絕

95 I appreciate it.：感謝你、謝謝你
同 Thanks so much，口語比較常用。

96 rest assured：放心、別擔心
Please rest assured that your son will be in good hands.
請放心，你兒子會被妥善照顧的。

97 conflict of interest：利益衝突

98 nor：也不
I didn't think too much about the case, nor do I intend to.
這個案我沒想太多，也不打算去多想。注意 nor 後面的主詞
和動詞要倒裝。

99 do (any) harm：造成傷害、傷害到

NOTE

100 either：也不，用於否定句；相對於肯定句的 **too**。

To tell you the truth, I don't like him either.

告訴你實話，我也不喜歡他。

101 sustain：支撐、維持、持續

Unless we find ways to differentiate, we won't be able to sustain the price war.

除非我們有辦法差異化，我們將無法持續打價格戰。

102 over the long run：長期下來、長遠來看

103 work on commission basis：以賺取佣金的方式做生意

104 exhibit：參展

105 fall into：在此是指「屬於」

106 straightforward：簡單的、直接了當的

Edward, please give me a straightforward answer.

Edward，請直接了當回答我。

107 maybe：或許、大概，等同 **perhaps**，多半用於句首。

注意不要把 maybe 與 may be 弄混了，may be 是「可能」的意思。

John may be out of town today. Maybe our meeting will be canceled.

John 今天可能到外地，或許我們的會議得取消了。

108 **see each other**：見面

109 **if we could be of any service to you**：如果我們還能幫上忙

Oliver, please feel free to call me if we could be of any service to you.

Oliver，如果我們還能幫上忙，請別客氣，儘管打電話給我。

110 **treat**：對待、看待

111 **earn**：掙得、贏來

Henry, about the bonus, you will have to earn it.

Henry，關於紅利，你必須靠自己掙來。

112 **have a drink**：喝酒或飲料的意思

113 **I'd love to**：我很樂意

I'd 在這裡是 I would 的縮寫。

114 **no exception**：不例外

He is always late. Today is no exception.

他老是遲到，今天也不例外。

Note

Lesson 8 — Advertising & Exhibitions

廣告與參展

課文重點① **Summary 1**

Despite the ever increasing importance of web marketing, most B2B firms would still adopt PR, advertising, trade shows, or product seminars as the major promotional methods for industrial products. For many distributors or dealers, the level of promotional support from the manufacturer also shows how important they are as a channel partner. Co-op promotion, either in the form of advertisement or exhibition, is a common practice.

近年來網路科技突飛猛進，網路行銷也很快成為重要競爭策略。然而在 B2B 模式下，多數企業仍舊採取傳統離線促銷推廣方式，比如公關活動、廣告、參展，或研討會。對於許多通路商來說，能得到供應廠商在推廣促銷上的贊助或密切配合極為重要。而聯手合作廣告或參展就成為一種常見的作法。

合作廣告與參展：co-op ad & trade shows 8-1

Lisa : **Marketing Manager, Sun Precision (Taiwan)**：行銷經理，臺灣

James : **Sales VP, Star Lab (Distributor, Australia)**：業務副總，澳洲總代理

Lisa : Hey, James, how's it going? I have good news for you. It is about our <u>promotion plan</u> for the coming year.

嘿 James，還好嗎？我有好消息告訴你，是關於我們明年的促銷計畫。

James : <u>Oh yeah?</u> <u>Sounds interesting,</u> what does it <u>look like</u>?

是喔？聽起來挺有趣的，計畫內容如何？

Lisa : Well, first we'll have one <u>co-op trade show</u> with you in each of March and September.

首先嘛，我們會在三月和九月各有一次合作參展。

James : Sounds great, how should we share the costs? Is it <u>fifty-fifty</u> as usual?

聽起來不錯哦，那成本要如何分攤？照往例各出一半嗎？

Lisa : Yes, it's fifty-fifty, however the costs of the <u>conferences</u> will be fully <u>on our account</u>.

是的，一半一半，不過，研討會的費用全部由本公司負擔。

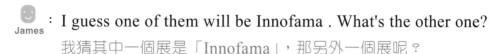

James : I guess one of them will be Innofama . What's the other one?

我猜其中一個展是「Innofama」，那另外一個展呢？

Lisa : Yes, one will be Innofama in March at Sydney Convention Center while the other will be Automeasure in September at the Brisbane Hilton.

是的，一個是三月在雪梨會議中心的「Innofama」，另外一個是九月在布里斯班希爾頓的「Automeasure」。

James : Besides trade shows, we also need to advertise in local trade publications. We have failed to do so for more than two years.

除了參展，我們還得在當地的產業刊物上刊登廣告，我們已有兩年以上沒登過廣告了。

Lisa : We didn't find the printed ad effective enough in recent years. You may want to try internet advertising from now on.

我們發現最近幾年，平面廣告效果並不好。從今以後，我們可能得試試看網路廣告了。

James : I'll have to discuss it with the team members and come back to you later.

我得先和業務團隊討論後再來找妳談。

NOTE

1 despite：儘管、雖然

Ricky, we will attend the seminar tomorrow, despite the bad weather.

Ricky，儘管天氣很糟糕，我們明天還是要去參加研討會。

2 ever increasing：不斷增加的

We were forced to cut down our marketing expenditures as a result of the ever increasing operating cost.

由於營運成本不斷增加，我們被迫得削減行銷支出。

3 web marketing：網路行銷

4 B2B firm：B2B 企業

B2B 為 Business to Business 的縮寫。

5 adopt：採用、採納

Nancy, we should adopt a more systematic scoring method for the daily incoming sales leads.

Nancy，針對每天進來的銷售線索，我們應該採用一種系統化評分方法。

6 PR：公關

為 Public Relations 的縮寫。

7 product seminar：產品研討會

8 distributor：代理商、配銷商

9 dealer：經銷商

NOTE

⑩ level：水準、水平、層次

Dell provides its customers with a high level of technical support.

Dell 提供高層次技術支援給客戶。

⑪ channel partner：通路夥伴，常指代理商或經銷商。

Ella, we have more than 50 channel partners in 45 countries worldwide.

Ella，全球 45 國家裡我們有超過 50 家的通路夥伴。

⑫ co-op promotion：聯合、合作促銷

指供應廠商與其客戶（多為通路夥伴）共同參展。co-op 是 co-operative 的縮寫。

Lily, we always do co-op promotion with our major channel partners.

Lily，我們都和我們的重要通路夥伴合作促銷。

⑬ form：形式

Eric, we'd rather show our appreciation to our customers in the form of more attractive business terms.

Eric，我們寧可用更好的交易條件，以對客戶的支持表達感謝之意。

⑭ common practice：常見作法、慣例

Offering our customers regular application seminars is a common practice in the industry.

在這行業裡，定期提供客戶應用技術研討會是常有的做法。

NOTE

⑮**promotion plan**：促銷計畫、推廣計畫

⑯**oh yeah?**：是嗎？你是這樣想的嗎？

是「Is it what you think?」的口語說法。

⑰**(it) sounds interesting**：聽起來挺有趣的

⑱**look like**：看起來像

I don't remember what the tower looks like.

我不記得那座塔是什麼樣子

⑲**co-op trade show**：聯合、合作展覽

Dennis, we'll be in a co-op trade show with our channel partner in Japan this Fall, in Tokyo.

Dennis，我們今年秋天會和日本的通路夥伴在東京共同參展。

⑳**fifty-fifty**：50-50，各分擔一半費用

Bob, since it's a joint event, I suggest we go fifty-fifty.

Bob，既然是共同辦活動，我建議我們各付一半費用。

㉑**conference**：研討會、討論會

較有規模的展會，會在展期中針對產業、技術、或個別廠商相關議題安排討論會。

㉒**on our account**：算在我們帳戶上、由我們支付

Alex, all the shipping expenses are on our account.

Alex，所有運輸費用都由我們支付。

NOTE

㉓ **besides**：此外、除了⋯之外

Roger, besides the trade shows that you mentioned, do you have any plans to hold technical seminars?

Roger，除了你提到的參展，你們打算舉辦技術研討會嗎？

㉔ **advertise**：刊登廣告

James, please check with Marcom and make sure that we're allowed to advertise on ECN next year.

James，請和 Marcom 確認明年我們可以在 ECN 上刊登廣告。

㉕ **trade publication**：行業、產業刊物

㉖ **fail to**：沒能做到、無法做到

Greg failed to finish the rolling forecast.

Greg 沒能完成滾動預估。

㉗ **printed ad**：平面印刷廣告

ad 是 advertisement 的縮寫。

㉘ **internet advertising**：網路廣告

也可說 web advertising。

㉙ **from now on**：從現在開始

Congratulations, Daniel! From now on, you're going to lead the entire Marcom team.

恭喜你，Daniel！從現在起，你將領導整個 Marcom 團隊。

NOTE

㉚**come back to you later**：稍後再來找你（談）

Janet, take a look at this report first and I'll come back to you later.

Janet，妳先看一下這份報告，我稍晚就來找妳談。

課文重點② **Summary 2**

For a B2B marketing or sales person, <u>participating</u> in a trade show is the best way to learn more about the industry, the market, the customers, the <u>applications</u>, the <u>competitors</u>, and many other things. It is also the most <u>effective</u> way to meet the <u>prospects</u> and communicate with them for possible future business. <u>Therefore</u>, in order to <u>get better results</u> from trade shows, the exhibiting firm has to make sure that each show is <u>well planned</u> <u>beforehand</u>, that all participating members at the <u>booth</u> - especially sales and FAEs - are well prepared, and that all leads are followed up quickly and effectively.

對一位 B2B 行銷業務人員來說，參展是一個最佳的學習成長機會。他們能在短短三五天內密集學著多了解產業運作、了解市場需求與動態、了解各種不同型態客戶和應用場合、同時也了解競爭對手和許多相關的事情。由於可以面對面直接與參觀者互動，參展也是去深入了解潛在客戶，並進行溝通以及獲取銷售線索的最佳場合。因此參展廠商必須在事前做好完整規劃，現場人員特別是業務與 FAE，一定得準備充分並在展後積極主動追蹤聯繫。

展會現場：at the show 8-2

> **Andy** : **Senior Account Manager, VT Precision (Taiwan)**：
> 資深客戶經理，臺灣
>
> **Phil** : **Engineer, Horizon Systems (Visitor)**：工程師，來賓
>
> **Denise** : **Engineer, Process Master (Visitor)**：工程師，來賓

Andy : Hello there, welcome. I'm Andy Wang. Here's my card. How may I help you?

哈囉，歡迎參觀！我叫 Andy Wang，這是我名片。能為您服務嗎？

Dr. Lee 解析

展會中最常見的情景，就是看見參觀者駐足在展位外觀看。此時負責接待的廠商人員最好能主動打招呼，傳達友善熱情。

Phil : Thanks Andy. I'm Phil Lang from Horizon Systems, Malaysia. Yes, I'm trying to find a force sensor for my company. I'm not sure if I can find it from your standard lines.

謝謝你，Andy，我是馬來西亞 Horizon Systems 的 Phil Lang。我在替公司找一種力感測器，不知道你們標準品裡是否有我想要的。

Dr. Lee 解析

> 展會是接觸準客戶、關鍵對象的最好時機，常常會碰到工程師看展找尋所需產品。

Andy : What's the application and the major <u>features</u>, as well as the technical specs required?

是哪種應用？需要有哪些主要特性和技術規格呢？

Dr. Lee 解析

> 許多工業產品跨多產業，問清楚應用場合方能快速進入商談核心。

Phil : It's for an <u>infusion pump</u> application. We are planning to develop an infusion pump using a <u>force sensor</u> or <u>strain gage</u> as the measuring device. <u>Feature-wise</u>, it has to be very small in size to save space and must have <u>high precision</u> to meet the medical requirements.

是用在輸注泵上的。我們打算用力感測器或應變計作為量測元件，開發一種輸注泵。特性是體積小省空間，而且精度要夠高能達到醫療要求。

Dr. Lee 解析

工業產品應用場合明確之後，就能帶出產品特性與技術規格等需求。

Andy : I see. The products you just saw here are our standard products only. We do have some <u>brochures</u> showing our <u>customized</u> sensors for <u>a wide variety of</u> applications including medical devices. You may want to <u>take a look</u> first. I'll be back with you soon.

了解。你剛才在展位上看到的全是我們標準產品，這兒有些產品說明小冊，介紹我們因應許多不同應用需求開發出來的客製化感測器，也包括醫療器材。你不妨先看看這些資料，我回頭再和你談談。

Dr. Lee 解析

通常展位上所展出的多是量大的標準品，客製化產品則以相關資訊提供參觀者檢視，或由在場人員接待。

Phil : Looks nice. OK, I'll <u>review</u> it right now. Thanks.

看起來很不錯。好，我就先瞧瞧，謝謝。

Andy : Hi there, how are you doing? My name is Andy Wang. This is my card. Did you see anything interesting here?

嗨，你好嗎？我是 Andy Wang，這是我的名片。有看到什麼您感興趣的嗎？

Dr. Lee 解析

展位上參觀者經常成群同時光顧，廠商接待人員以一對多情形很正常，業務 Andy 現在得服務 Phil 和 Denise 二位參觀者。

Denise: Hi, I'm Denise White from Process Master, New York, U.S.A. Yes, I found your sensor lines on the internet before. I <u>was very interested in</u> your <u>digital damped transducers</u> at that time. It's so good to visit the show as I didn't expect to be here until <u>the day before yesterday</u> when I was told to come here to attend to some <u>local project business</u>.

嗨，我是美國紐約 Process Master 的 Denise White。我先前有從網路上看到你們的各式感測器。那時我對你們的數位式阻尼傳感器很有興趣。能來參觀這次展覽真好，因為直到前天我被告知得來談一項本地標案之前，都還沒想到會有機會來參觀。

Dr. Lee 解析

現今 B2B 模式下，絕大多數客戶會在線上先行搜尋所需產品，取得足夠資訊後再進行實質接觸。對買方採購決策人員來說，參觀展會依舊是最重要也是最實際有效的接觸方式之一。

Andy: I'm glad that you came. What industry is Process Master in? Process automation or automatic machine building?

真高興你能來。你們在哪一個行業？製程自動化或自動機器製造？。

Dr. Lee 解析

同樣的，了解應用場合是第一步。

Denise: Actually both. We are a <u>system integration</u> company <u>specializing</u> in high speed <u>industrial measuring</u>. Meanwhile we also make automatic machines <u>on a customized basis</u>.

事實上都有。我們是一家系統整合公司，專門從事高速工業量測。同時我們也接些客製化自動機器的開發製作生意。

Dr. Lee 解析

應用範圍越廣，表示生意機會也越多。

Andy: Awesome! You just mentioned that you're looking for digital damped transducers. Is it for <u>stand-alone</u> machines or for <u>in-line</u> continuous measuring? And why only the digital version? We have both <u>analog</u> and digital dampers.

真讚。你剛提到正在找數位式阻尼傳感器，那是要用在獨立機臺上或是產線上連續量測用的？為什麼只找數位式的呢？類比式的和數位式的我們都有。

Dr. Lee 解析

更精確了解應用場合。

Denise : It's for an in-line continuous application. It's more <u>convenient</u> for us to use digital signals to connect with our production network. <u>Moreover</u>, it's easier to <u>maintain</u> and <u>calibrate</u> the systems. <u>Nevertheless</u>, we also need analog dampers for stand-alone machines.

那是線上連續量測用的。用數位信號連接我們的生產網路會方便許多,而且維護或校正起來更簡單。但說到獨立機臺,我們也需要用到類比式的。

Dr. Lee 解析

在交談中就能確認參觀者(搜尋者)的細項需求。

Andy : I see. You may want to play with the <u>laptop</u> here first and watch our application video for the damped transducers. <u>I'll be with you in a minute</u>.

了解。你可以先在這筆電上瀏覽一下阻尼傳感器的應用影片,我很快就回來和你聊聊。

Dr. Lee 解析

在現今網路時代,展出廠商能運用各種網路科技提供更廣更深入的專業服務。

Denise : OK, thanks.

好的,謝謝。

Phil : Hi, Andy, I'm finished with all this literature, and it was very informative. I wonder if you could mail a few sets to me after the show? I'm glad that I found many medical applications using your customized products. And I believe we'll be able to make good use of them.

嗨 Andy，我看完這些介紹資料了，內容很不錯。能否請你在展覽結束後郵寄給我一些資料？很開心我找到你們不少客製化產品可用在醫療應用上，我想我們會好好利用這些資訊的。

工程師訪客特別注重相關資訊的收集與了解。

Andy : That's good. Did you find any possible solutions to your infusion pump project? Or do you want to talk with one of our FAEs on a specific applications problem?

那很好。針對輸注泵，你有找到任何可能的解決方案嗎？或是你有特定的應用問題想問我們應用工程團隊呢？

工業產品參展廠商在現場必定有應用工程師支援，有必要可隨時支援業務人員。

Phil : Yes, I will come back later to discuss with your engineer in relation to some technical issues. I need to look around first.

會的，我稍後會回來和他們討論一些技術問題。我得先四處去
看看展覽。

Dr. Lee 解析

可先大致逛過一次再回頭鎖定議題討論。

Andy : Sure, please do. I'll be here <u>all day long</u> till 4 p.m. You can also talk to any of those guys with the yellow <u>badge</u> on their shirt. They are our FAEs.

當然，請務必再光臨。我下午四點以前一直會在這裡，你也可以找任何一位佩戴黃色名牌的應用工程師談。

Dr. Lee 解析

找對人討論很重要。

Phil : <u>Got it.</u> Thanks a lot.

好的，真謝謝你。

Andy : Hey Denise, <u>are you done with</u> those videos? Did you find them interesting?

嘿 Denise，那些影片看完了嗎？覺得有趣嗎？

Dr. Lee 解析

Andy 又適時來與 Denise 繼續討論。

Denise: Not yet finished, but I did find something very interesting about the analog dampers. It may help improve the speed and the accuracy of our checking machines.

還沒看完。不過我發現類比阻尼傳感器很有趣的特性，那應該能幫助我們改善檢測設備的速度和精度。

Dr. Lee 解析

對參觀者來說，最大收獲莫過於能順利在展會裡找到解決問題的方法。

Andy: Wonderful ! Did you have a chance to talk to any of our FAEs? They are all very experienced with the dampers. By the way, may I have one of your cards?

太好了。你和我們應用工程師談過了嗎？他們對於阻尼傳感器非常有經驗。對了，可以給我一張名片嗎？

Dr. Lee 解析

交換名片還是很重要的溝通技巧。

Denise: Oh, I'm sorry that I forgot. Here it is. I guess I'll visit you again later, maybe tomorrow, to discuss in detail with your engineers. I need to run for an appointment 10 minutes from now. I'll talk to you.

哎呀！抱歉，我都忘了。這是我的名片。我想明天我會再來和你們工程師討論細節。十分鐘後我還有個約，我得趕過去了，

我們再聊。

Dr. Lee 解析

能夠重複或持續討論也是展會的重要功能之一。

Andy ： Cool, I'll see you tomorrow.
好，明天見。

❶ **participate**：參加、參與

By participating in trade shows, marketing people collect first-hand market information.

藉由參展，行銷人員能夠收集到第一手市場資訊

❷ **application**：應用（場合）

I'm sorry, Lisa. We have quite a few crystals for mobile communications. What's your specific application?

抱歉，Lisa，我們有好幾顆石英晶片可用在行動通訊上，請問貴公司的特定應用是什麼？

❸ **competitor**：競爭者

❹ **effective**：有效的

Mia, please research to see if web marketing is more effective than traditional off-line marketing.

Mia，請妳去研究一下，網路行銷是否比傳統離線式行銷有效。

NOTE

⑤prospect：潛在客戶、有機會開發的客戶

⑥therefore：所以、因此

Therefore, we have to be more accurate working out our monthly forecasts for key components.

所以，我們關鍵零組件的月預估值得做得更精確才行。

⑦get better result：有好結果、得到好結果

Barbara, we must get better results from the two exhibitions that we attend this year.

Barbara，我們必須從今年參加的兩個展會中得到更好的成果。

⑧well planned：計畫周詳的

Andy, about the show in March, make sure that everything is well planned.

Andy，關於三月的展，你得確定一切都規劃好了。

⑨beforehand：事前、事先

Tom, about the printed ad on Metal Today, I should have reported to you beforehand.

Tom，關於在 Metal Today 上刊登平面廣告，我應該事先向你報告的。

⑩booth：（展會的）攤位

Megan, don't forget our booth number is C8110.

Megan，別忘了我們攤位編號是 C8110。

⑪ **Hello there (or "Hi there")**：哈囉，你好（嗨，你好）

是一種常用的口語化打招呼說法，尤其在還不知對方名字情況下或還有點距離時用。

⑫ **standard line**：指標準產品系列

⑬ **feature**：特性、特色

Ian, while selecting components, most people focus on the specifications, features, and the cost.

Ian，使用者選擇零組件時大多只比較規格、特性，和成本。

⑭ **infusion pump**：輸液泵、注射器幫浦

⑮ **force sensor**：力感應器

⑯ **strain gage**：應變計

⑰ **feature-wise**：在…特性上

Feature-wise, our 17-4 PH stainless steel is much better than 316 stainless steel for corrosion resistance.

在抗腐蝕性上，我們的 17-4 PH 不鏽鋼，要比 316 不鏽鋼好太多了。

⑱ **high precision**：高精確度

Ted, be careful with those high precision and fragile instruments.

Ted，小心操作這些高精度但易損壞的儀器。

NOTE

⑲ **brochure**：介紹性的小冊子
多為印刷品，介紹公司、產品、或應用技術。

⑳ **customized**：客製化的、專為客戶量身訂做的
The sales revenue of our customized business accounts for 25 % of our total revenue.
我們客製化營收占總營收 25%。

㉑ **a wide variety of**：多樣的、多種的
The hotel offers a wide variety of foods.
這旅館提供很多種口味的食物。

㉒ **take a look**：看一看、瀏覽

㉓ **review**：檢討、審視
Hey guys, bear in mind our one-on-one account review starts next Monday.
各位請注意：下週一開始要做一對一的客戶檢討。

㉔ **be interested in**：對⋯有興趣
Helen is interested in web page design.
Helen 對網頁設計很有興趣

㉕ **digital damped transducers**：數位式阻尼傳感器，常用於動態重量量測。

㉖ **the day before yesterday**：前天

㉗ local：本地的、當地的

Nathan, both XTE and AXC are local crystal manufacturers.

Nathan，XTE 和 AXC 都是本地石英生產廠商。

㉘ project business：專案生意，通常為標案

Monica, the project business you won last week bailed us out of the performance doldrums.

Monica，妳上星期拿到的專案訂單讓我們走出業績低潮。

bail out 協助脫離困境；doldrums 停滯、低潮。

㉙ system integration：系統整合

Systec has been famous for its excellent performance in manu-facturing systems integration.

Systec 一直以在製造系統整合領域中優秀表現聞名。

㉚ specialize：專精於、專門於。

Matt is an experienced FAE specializing in process automation.

Matt 是一位專精在製程自動化的老經驗 FAE。

㉛ industrial measuring：工業量測

如力（重量）、扭力、壓力、溫度、厚薄度、平坦度、黏度等等。

㉜ on a customized basis：在客製化原則上

Jack, regarding your query last week, we're able to do it on a customized basis.

Jack，回應你上星期的問題，我們有辦法用客製化的方式處理。

NOTE

㉝ **stand-alone**：獨立的、單機的

Steven, is the new analytical balance in Lab 12 a stand-alone one?

Steven，在 12 號實驗室裡那臺新的分析天平，是單機使用的嗎？

㉞ **in-line**：線上的、屬於生產線上的

Chris, when will you calibrate those in-line IR thermometers along the forging line?

Chris，你何時會校正那些在鍛造線上的紅外線溫度儀？

㉟ **analog**：類比式的

㊱ **convenient**：方便、便利

㊲ **moreover**：而且、此外

I think the price of that multi-meter is reasonable, and moreover, the quality is really good.

我認為那多用電表價格合理，而且品質又很好。

㊳ **maintain**：維護

The new testing machine we installed in our R&D lab is too sensitive and is very difficult to maintain.

我們研發實驗室裡新安裝的那臺測試機太靈敏，維護起來很困難。

㊴ **calibrate**：校正、調校

NOTE

⓵ **nevertheless**：然而、不過

I know that you guys have been working days and nights on this. Nevertheless, we still have tons of jobs to finish.

我理解大家已經有好一陣子沒日沒夜在忙這件事，不過我們還有成堆的工作得完成。

⓶ **laptop**：筆電 laptop PC 或 notebook PC

⓷ **I'll be with you in a minute**：「我很快就回來（找你）」。

常用的口語。

⓸ **I'm finished with**：我已經做完某件事、準備好了

I'm finished with the calibration.

我已校正完畢。

⓹ **literature**：印刷品，包括企業內與產品服務相關，或年度財報等印刷品。

Sandra, please send two sets of your product literature to me ASAP.

Sandra，請盡快寄二套產品印刷文宣給我。

⓺ **informative**：很有內容的、具知識性的

Sam, the technical seminar yesterday was very informative.

Sam，昨天的技術研討會很有內容。

NOTE

㊻wonder if：不知是否

I wonder if you could give me a ride to Metro station.

不知是否可以搭你的便車去捷運站？

㊼make good use of：好好利用、善加利用

Guys, now you each have a nice new iPad. Please make good use of it at work, of course.

各位，現在你們每人都有一臺新的 iPad，好好利用啊！不用說，當然是用在工作上！

㊽FAE：應用工程師

為 Field Applications Engineer 的縮寫。

㊾specific：特定的、明確的

Christine, please be more specific.

Christine，請說得更明確些。

㊿look around：四處逛逛看看

Mike, before the meeting, I'm going to take you to look around our factory.

Mike，會議之前，我先帶你在工廠裡四處看一看。

51all day long：一整天

Oh thank God, the courier van has arrived. We've been waiting all day long for those labels.

感謝老天爺，快遞貨車到了。我們等這批標籤一整天了。

52badge：識別證、識別徽章

53 Got it：知道了、懂了

一種常用的口語講法。

54 are you done with：你已經完成…了嗎

Frank, are you done with your report?

Frank，你報告完成了沒？

55 not yet：還沒、尚未

I'm not done yet.

我還沒好（做完、吃完）。

56 help improve：有助於改善…

口語中 help 後緊接原形動詞而省略 to。

Sandy, the huge order from HP helped improve our utilization rate significantly.

Sandy，HP 的大單大幅改善我們的產能使用率。

57 experienced：很有經驗的、經驗豐富的

Ryan is the most experienced sales in our team.

Ryan 是我們團隊裡最有經驗的業務。

58 by the way：附帶問、順便提

相當於開場白：「對了…」。

By the way Frank, did you finish calibrating the meters?

對了，Frank，你校正完儀表了嗎？

59 may I have one of your cards?：能給我你的名片嗎？

NOTE

⑥here it is.：這給你

回應上句說：「這是我的名片，請多多指教」。

⑥maybe：或許、大概

Because of the incident, maybe we should start to find another source for OCXO.

由於這事件，或許我們得開始找另一家 OCXO 廠商。

⑥I need to run：我得離開

並不一定真用跑的，指表示得離開到別處的說法，等同 I have to leave。

國家圖書館出版品預行編目資料

B2B企業英語會話. 行銷篇／李純白著.
— 初版. — 臺北市：五南, 2015.11
　　　面；　公分
ISBN 978-957-11-8340-4（平裝）

1.商業英文　2.會話

805.188　　　　　　104018873

1XOF

B2B企業英語會話～行銷篇

作　　者 — 李純白

發 行 人 — 楊榮川

總 編 輯 — 王翠華

主　　編 — 朱曉蘋

封面設計 — 劉好音

出 版 者 — 五南圖書出版股份有限公司

地　　址：106台北市大安區和平東路二段339號4樓

電　　話：(02)2705-5066　　傳　　真：(02)2706-6100

網　　址：http://www.wunan.com.tw

電子郵件：wunan@wunan.com.tw

劃撥帳號：01068953

戶　　名：五南圖書出版股份有限公司

法律顧問　林勝安律師事務所　林勝安律師

出版日期　2015年11月初版一刷

定　　價　新臺幣400元